Her lips took me back to delirium, and her hands created new excitement under my shirt. I felt for her hips but didn't have the nerve to explore further. Anyway, what I really wanted was what she was doing to me.

She yanked down my gym shorts and panties, turning them into shackles around my ankles. I was crazed with desire but also with fear — who else had a key to the towel room door?

Jaws didn't give me much time to wonder. Her fingers went where it counted, touching, teasing, stroking, now gentle, now demanding, making me care about nothing in the universe except what was happening here, here, here. She knew what she was doing, and I was eager and inexperienced and overwhelmed, and in no time at all I was clinging to her to keep myself upright while wave after rapturous wave pounded through me in violent release.

Jaws kissed me on the forehead. "We better get out of here."

I collected myself shakily. Jaws waited while I showered. I was still pretty dazed when I reappeared, and she seemed quite pleased with what she had done. "I may have to keep you after school again tomorrow," she said.

COURTED

by
Celia Cohen

THE NAIAD PRESS, INC.
1997

Printed in the United States of America on acid-free paper
First Edition

Editor: Christine Cassidy
Cover designer: Bonnie Liss (Phoenix Graphics)
Typesetter: Sandi Stancil

Library of Congress Cataloging-in-Publication Data

Cohen, Celia, 1953 –
    Courted / Celia Cohen.
        p.   cm.
    ISBN 1-56280-166-X (p)
    I. Title.
PS3553.04188C68   1997
813'.54—dc21
                                                    96-45490
                                                    CIP

About the Author

Celia Cohen is a newspaper writer who lives in Delaware. She is the author of *Smokey O* and *Payback*.

CHAPTER ONE

At first the other cops were jealous when they found out I was the one assigned to the security detail for Alessandra de Ville.

To the tennis world she was known simply as Alie, which was pronounced like *alley*. At twenty years old, she was the hottest prospect on the women's tour.

Alie was the only child of a self-made tycoon who got obscenely rich by solving a national pet peeve. Papa de Ville did it by creating a glue that let people peel off those stubborn little white price stickers with ease and without leaving a trace. Before that he was scuffling through life, working as a counterman at a 24-hour-a-day diner. When his shift was over, he experimented obsessively with his glue until he got it right.

Papa de Ville's creation was a sensation. The retailers fell into line one by one for his stickers and paid his price. Overnight he went from picking up tips on the counter to picking up tips on the stock market. He was the Guru of Glue, and he was worth millions. Best of all, his discovery was the sort that let him remain anonymous. No one knew who Oscar de Ville was, and he could do whatever he wanted.

What he wanted to do more than anything was lavish attention on his daughter. Papa de Ville was on his third wife, but he never wavered about Alie, who was well-suited to make the most of it. Like father, like daughter.

Alie had eyes as dark and melting as a puppy's, lips like silk and the soul of a jewel thief. When she saw something she wanted, she took it. Nobody seemed to mind. It was an entitlement that came with being born blonde.

Alie was the marquee name for the first women's professional tennis tournament ever to be staged in Hillsboro, the forgettable little city in central Pennsylvania where I worked on the police force. Papa de Ville grew up without distinction among Hillsboro's residents, numbered at 23,507 and shrinking by the 1990 census. Although he left long ago, even before the dog days at the diner, he was putting up the money for the tournament. It wasn't out of any sense of civic pride, but because he

2

wanted to show everybody what a big shot he had become.

The tournament was an exhibition match, meaningless in the standings. It was one of those squirrelly little sidelights that didn't mean much to the pros, and they wouldn't have come at all if Papa de Ville hadn't made the prize so rich. It wasn't enough to attract the reigning legends like Steffi Graf or Monica Seles, but some of the teen sensations like Martina Hingis, the Australian Open champion, and Venus Williams were signed up, and so was Lindsay Davenport, the U.S. gold medal winner at the Olympic games in Atlanta. Most of them weren't even bothering to bring their coaches along, although the full complement of overprotective tennis parents like Papa de Ville would be there. News coverage was expected to be sparse.

It was a big deal to Hillsboro, though. This was a place without much of anything, not since the mines gave out decades ago. It muddled along amid barren foothills, relying for life support on a small campus called Hillsboro College, a regional hospital and a surprisingly prosperous paper mill beside a rushing stream.

Papa wanted this exhibition tournament so much that he donated money to the college to build stands for its tennis courts so it could host the match.

My first assignment was to take Alie to the College Inn to get settled before a banquet there in the evening.

The inn was probably the classiest establishment within the Hillsboro city limits. It was located on the outskirts of the college campus. Part of it was a century old, quaint with antique furnishings, gaping fireplaces and a tea room so formal you still expected to see women wearing delicate white gloves. The inn hosted a lawn croquet tournament every year and had the only public grass tennis court in the state.

About five years ago Hillsboro College decided to market itself for business conferences, so it built a convention center and the College Inn added a modern wing. The new rooms had computer ports, telephones and televisions in the bathrooms, refrigerators and microwaves. It had a state-of-the-art fitness club and a newsstand that pledged it could get you any major newspaper in the country — just let them know when you made your reservations.

Alie had requested a room in the new wing. Papa de Ville had called later to make sure the Presidential Suite was reserved for her. He wouldn't be staying there himself. He had contacted the local hospital and arranged to rent a condo at the Buena Vista Country Club normally made available to visiting doctors. Papa de Ville intended to do some heavy-duty entertaining in Hillsboro to make up for his scruffy childhood.

This tennis tournament was like an extra Christmas. The mayor was determined nothing would go wrong, and he ordered the police chief to use every cop for security. The campus police force was going to pitch in too.

Cops usually hate these celebrity security assignments. We didn't get many of them, just for the occasional performing artist appearing at the college or a politician coming through town to campaign. Bonnie Raitt had been through earlier in the year, and a couple years ago the college hosted a debate in

4

the U.S. Senate race between Democrat Harris Wofford, the incumbent who lost, and Republican Rick Santorum. The security detail was always disruptive and occasionally demeaning. A rock band had pushed us to the limit last spring. We were treated like the hired help, carrying bags and holding elevators open and tracking down a Chinese restaurant willing to deliver moo shu shrimp at two in the morning.

Alie de Ville's presence got our attention, though, and the whole force suddenly became very serious about security. After reaching the quarterfinals at Wimbledon, Alie had won back-to-back tournaments in Italy and Poland, and her picture was on the cover of *Sports Illustrated*. She was wearing the most daring little tennis skirt you ever did see, caught by the wind just so, in a modern treatment of that famous rendition of Marilyn Monroe. The issue was threatening to outsell the swimsuit edition.

Almost every cop was angling for Alie's security detail. Fortunately for me, Captain Randie Wilkes was in charge of the assignments. We had a special bond, going back to the days when I was a moody, misdirected kid and she was a young patrolwoman who coaxed me into playing in the Police Softball League for girls. She put me on security for Alie, even though I was pretty junior. I was twenty-four with only three years on the force.

Sergeant Arnold Cranshaw, who had perpetual desk duty because of an impressive Jello-like gut we called "The Beer Belly Polka," couldn't contain himself when he heard. "A blonde like that, and she goes to you, Kotter? What a waste!" he said.

Waste, hell. Like most of the cops in this

5

repressive little city, Sergeant Cranshaw was too out of it to know what Alie's appetites were — or what mine were, for that matter.

I didn't care one bit that Alie was making her living by looking like every man's dreamboat. Alie and I were going to get along fine.

I helped myself to some gum from the pack on Cranshaw's desk. Then I gave him one of those impudent grins cops are famous for. It's not true you learn how to smirk at the academy; either you're born with the knack or you'll never make the force.

"Just listen to yourself, Sarge. Maybe Captain Wilkes wanted someone who could keep her mind on her job," I said.

"Who wants a blonde like Alie de Ville on their mind? I want her on my lap!" Cranshaw leered.

"Lap, Sarge? When was the last time you had one?"

"Kotter, that sounds a hell of a lot like insubordination."

"Why is it whenever I tell the truth, it's insubordination?" I said and beat it out of there.

I slipped into Randie's office to pay my respects. She looked up, and I was struck as always by the alertness in her eyes, the sharpness that said she was ready for anything — confronting a killer, comforting a lost child or outsmarting a practical joker.

Randie was what cynical employers called a twofer. She was the highest ranking African-American woman in the department, and it was only a matter of time before she was promoted even higher. She was thirty-six, and everyone on the force expected her to be chief before she turned forty.

Randie's full name was Ruth Diane Wilkes. When

her little sister mispronounced her first name as Roof, Randi took to calling herself by her initials, R.D. Her playmates quickly transformed it into Randie. It stuck for life.

Randie was a cop's cop. Her walls were decorated with all manner of awards for police work and community service. She had been beaten up working undercover on a case against a serial killer who preyed on prostitutes. She had commanded a regional task force that flushed out a rogue cop who was robbing banks. She had coached a girls' softball team to a state championship — as I could have told anyone without looking at the plaque. I played on it.

"Hey, Captain," I said.

"Take that gum out of your mouth. You look like a street urchin."

I did as I was told. It was never wise to buck Randie Wilkes.

"Nice suit," she said.

"Thanks." I was wearing civilian clothes for security duty — dark blue slacks and jacket. Even when I was out of uniform, I couldn't seem to tear myself away from standard police colors. "The Beer Belly Polka thinks this security assignment is being wasted on me."

"Is it?"

"Only to the point that I already owe you my soul, so why do anything else for me?"

"Because it keeps you in line."

It was true. It did. I was difficult to motivate. "You don't have to remind me," I said.

"Don't I?"

I gave her the insolent cop grin but otherwise conceded her point. "I'm heading out to the airport."

"Already? It's early yet."

The Hill County Airport wasn't exactly your thriving hub of metropolitan air traffic. Normally it had one scheduled flight in the morning and one scheduled flight in the afternoon, both USAir. The airline had added an extra afternoon and an evening flight to accommodate the tournament. I'd been told to expect Alie on the first afternoon arrival.

"I thought I'd get the car washed on the way out," I said.

Randie fixed me with a half-mocking, half-patronizing look that never failed to make me feel twelve years old again. "It's a police car. It's not a Porsche," she said. "Surely you don't think you can impress an international tennis star with a clean police car, do you?"

I shrugged. Randie was beating me up pretty good, which was not unusual. It was time to keep my mouth shut. I was one of the few cops who personally appreciated the right to remain silent.

"I thought you had your eye on the new clerk at the Rising Moon," Randie said. The Rising Moon was a women's bookstore near the college campus.

"I do. This is different."

The telephone rang, and I waited through a short conversation. Randie hung up and said, "It doesn't look like you're going to have time for that car wash."

"Why not?"

"Alie de Ville is waiting for you at the airport."

"What!"

"You heard me."

"But the flight isn't due in —"

"It seems Papa de Ville sprang for a private jet."

I went pale. "Nobody told me. The tournament officials said —"

"Then they were wrong, weren't they?"

"Fuck it. I'm outta here."

Such is the life of being a cop. You're never summoned until after the damage is done.

I lit out of Randie's office and made for the cruiser. I flipped on the lights and the siren, going like a banshee for the airport. The other cars headed for the shoulders, bailing right and left out of the way. Usually this was one of the joys of the profession, but I was too put out to care.

As I made the turn onto Airport Road, I cut off a van painted in the red and gold colors of Hillsboro College. It carried the women's tennis team, drafted by tournament officials to be part of the welcoming crew later in the afternoon. I caught a lucky break to get ahead of them. Every single one of those tennis players had lust in her heart for Alie de Ville. If I didn't get there first, they'd mob her.

I screamed into the airport and killed the siren and the lights. As I pulled up to the curb at the sign for arriving flights, I saw Alie and a considerable pile of luggage. She was waiting there with Sam Van Doren, the sergeant in charge of the security detail.

They did not look like a happy pair. Sam was standing as rigidly as if the departmental brass were working him over, and Alie looked icy beside him. Her arms were folded, her left hip jutted one direction and her right foot the other.

Still, I could not help but admire how her white shorts, so dazzling in the sunlight, clung to her hips and thighs, hugging her like a jealous lover. Nor could I ignore the way her cropped white T-shirt rose with each vexatious breath, offering a teasing peep show of tanned midriff. It was also impossible to miss the sparkle in her hair, so light and so fine.

Holy bombshell. I breathed deeply, as though Alie could turn the air into perfume, but all I got was the staleness inside the police car.

I parked and jumped out. Sam said, "Ms. de Ville, this is —"

"I don't care who she is. She's late," Alie hissed.

In the microsecond before I got mad, I was pleased to note that Alie's voice was as coarse as her body was classic. The gods in their cosmic irony had left at least something to be improved upon.

I never got to decide what I wanted to say to her. Sam warned me to silence with a ferocious glare, so I simply watched as Alie blew by on her long, muscled legs, yanked open the cruiser's back door and swiveled herself in, her white shorts pulling taut over all the right places. She slammed the door and stared straight ahead.

Sam grimaced. "Kotter, don't you dare say a word to her. The mayor will have our badges if any of these tennis players don't like their treatment — and that goes double for Alie de Ville."

"She's got one hell of a nerve."

"Well, she can. She's Alie de Ville, and we're not."

"I'm just supposed to put up with it?"

"Damn it, Kotter, I mean it!"

"Okay, Sam, okay."

There was no sense letting this get to me.

Otherwise, it was going to be a very long week. I was stuck with Princess Charming.

Anyway, there were worse things than having a pretty woman order me around.

CHAPTER TWO

I shifted the police car into gear and started rolling just as the college van pulled up with the women's tennis team. They were going to be vastly disappointed. I was content to leave them as Sam's problem, not mine.

"Is there a place in this town to get a good massage?" Alie asked, her unmanageable voice catching me by surprise all over again. It came from too far down in her throat. I figured I could get used to it, though — sort of like developing a fondness for cheap wine once you get drunk enough. It starts to suit your mood.

"Sure is," I said. Cops normally know everything about the city where they work, but in this case I was speaking from personal experience.

The most soothing hands around belonged to Julie Nemo, who just happened to be Randie Wilkes' woman. They were already together when I met them as a kid. I got massages for birthdays, Christmases and other special occasions.

Julie Nemo was gorgeous. She was tall and bronze and catlike, and her moods and expressions were so animated that she rarely had to speak to be understood. It was a nice contrast to Randi, who could batter you with words.

Julie was a physical therapist, personal trainer and masseuse, working out of the Buena Vista Country Club, where Papa de Ville was staying. It was on the other side of town, maybe fifteen minutes away, less if you're in a cop car and feeling frisky.

"Then take me there," Alie said. "I could use one."

I'd had about enough of this attitude. "Hey, I'm a cop, not a cabbie."

"You can still drive, can't you?"

"All right, but I'm going to wait outside and keep the meter running."

I glanced at the rear view mirror for her reaction, expecting to see storm clouds in her eyes. Instead, she was looking rather sunny — amused even. Maybe Alie de Ville liked a little sass.

I called the police desk on the car radio and asked to be patched through to Captain Wilkes. "The subject would like an immediate appointment with Nemo," I said. "Can you arrange?"

There was a pause, and I knew Randie wasn't any happier about this prima donna demand than I was. I also knew she would come through, and she did.

"Ten-four," she said tersely.

I headed for the country club. "You'll be on the massage table in half an hour," I said.

"Good."

I took another look in the rear view mirror. Alie was stretching, her arms reaching for the roof and pulling that short T-shirt up to display her taut midsection. Her back arched, and her nipples became silhouetted against the light fabric. It was sexy as hell.

Then I saw her eyes watching me in the mirror. She had found me out, for sure. Her features melted into a self-satisfied smile that had nothing to do with me.

"What's your name?" she asked.

"Kotter."

"What's your first name?"

"Officer Kotter."

"All right, be like that. You can call me Ms. de Ville."

"I wouldn't have it any other way, ma'am."

Alie sighed in disgust. "*Officer* Kotter. How old are you?"

"Twenty-four. I've been on the force three years."

"Well, I'm twenty. I've been on the pro tour four years."

"I'd have to be a hermit in a cave not to know that."

"Usually when I get to a new town, the police escort is a male musclehead."

"Maybe we do better detective work here."

She giggled. "It's hard to believe people don't know, but they never seem to."

"Maybe they got the wrong impression from that cover on *Sports Illustrated*."

She giggled again. "That was supposed to be a candid picture, but they made me stand in front of a fan for about a million shots."

"How come you're traveling alone? I thought tennis pros had a whole army supporting them."

"We do. I do. Coach, trainer, father, friends, security guard, sometimes even a cook, you name it. But after six weeks in Europe, I was sick of everything. I just wanted to be by myself for a little while and chill out."

We were driving through what passed for Hillsboro's downtown district — typical for a college town. There were a couple of coffee shops and ice cream parlors, bars with live music, pizza places and T-shirt stores, as well as the usual mix of drug stores, hardware store, clothing shops, movie house, real estate and doctors' offices and one dentist's place with a faulty alarm system that drove the police force crazy. It all looked fairly quaint, actually, because most of the storefronts hadn't been changed in decades. You could live here, all right, but if you wanted some variety, you'd have to drive to a bigger city for a mall.

Alie yawned. "What do people do for fun in this place? It looks pretty dead."

"Well, we don't have Broadway or the Eiffel Tower here, but there's enough to do if you know where to look."

"And you do?"

"I'm a cop. Of course, I do."

"So you'll take me there?"

"Negative. The drinking age is twenty-one in this state."

"So?"

"So you're not going."

"We'll see about that," Alie said darkly. The nasty screech in her voice sounded like a witch's curse, and I found myself shrugging, as if to ward it off. This babe was not to be trifled with.

I wheeled into the grand entrance of the Buena Vista Country Club, marked by two pretentious white pillars with lion statues roaring on the top of them. A canopy of broad, leafy tree limbs overhung the roadway, which rolled through manicured grounds. Alie perked up as we entered. Obviously she was at home in a place like this.

I eased the cruiser into a no-parking zone near the doorway of the clubhouse and killed the engine. Being a cop meant never having to worry about parking.

I got out of the car and waited a moment, giving Alie the time to figure out she was in a back seat with no door handles — a little gimmick for foiling escapes. She couldn't leave unless I let her.

Eventually she looked at me through the back

door window and gave a little smile of surrender. I had seen it before — on television after she lost a dogged, take-no-prisoners tennis match to Steffi Graf. I wished I could see it in bed.

I let her out. "Cute," she said.

"I bet you say that to all the girls."

Alie laughed. "You know, you're pretty funny for a cop."

"Ah, you're just used to the muscleheads."

She waited for me to open the clubhouse door for her. Naturally I did. She breezed by me without a word of thanks. The queen was in her element.

I waved to the receptionist and guided Alie through the lobby, which offered half-paneling to appeal to the men, multiple floral arrangements for the women and the sort of furniture found in the best hotels. We were on moneyed ground here.

Julie Nemo's quarters were toward the end of a long hallway, near the fitness center and racquetball courts. We entered her anteroom, where she was seated at her desk, waiting for us.

She stood up and gave me an affectionate hug. "Kotter! How's it going?"

"Good, Julie. Thanks for seeing us." I turned toward Alie to do the introductions, but she was looking stunned. Obviously she wasn't used to anybody else being greeted before she was gushed over.

I gave her the cop's grin. She gave me hooded eyes.

"Julie, this is Ms. de Ville," I said, knowing perfectly well that protocol required me to present Julie to Alie, not Alie to Julie. I didn't care. I was playing for keeps.

17

"A pleasure," Julie murmured, her voice as decorous as a lady in waiting. I loved the contrast to Alie's.

Julie sent Alie into the back to get ready for her massage. "She's a looker, isn't she?"

"You bet. Sorry to bust in on you with such short notice. Was it a problem?"

"A little. I had to reschedule Mrs. Bentley, the wife of the country club's treasurer. I'll probably be giving her free massages till Christmas to make sure she's pacified. Fortunately she's a tennis fan." Julie smiled. "She acted a little put out, but she'll be bragging to all her friends she was bumped from the massage table by Alie de Ville."

"Thanks, Julie."

"Don't mention it. What are friends for? Well, I better get ready for her. Make yourself comfortable, Kotter. I've got coffee, juice, sodas and muffins if you want any. The muffins are low-fat, by the way."

I picked up one of the women's beauty and fitness magazines that Julie kept around and paged through it for the pictures of women doing athletic activities in skimpy clothing. This was my idea of cheesecake.

I was memorizing the curve of the hip of a rollerblader when I heard the door to the back open. I looked up. There stood Alie, wearing nothing but a thick green and gold towel. She had it wrapped around herself in such a low, immodest way that it exposed her breasts above her nipples. I took as long a look as I dared, which was not nearly long enough. I stood up awkwardly, assuming she had come out because she wanted me to do something.

"Oh! Wrong door," she said sweetly. She stood

there another moment, wearing a brazen smile to go with the towel, and then she was gone.

Wrong door, hell. Alie knew just what she was doing. If she thought she could get to me that way, she was damn right.

CHAPTER THREE

The massage took the edge off Alie. In fact, it took so much off that she folded herself into some sort of personal cocoon and didn't say another word to me. If I felt like a servant before, I felt like furniture now.

This babe had two speeds: stop and go. I wasn't sure which one was more infuriating.

Alie oozed into the back seat of the patrol car and looked vacantly out the window. I drove her to the College Inn and let her out. She slinked inside without looking back, her hips pumping against those white shorts, and left the doorman and me to deal with her luggage. So what else was new?

I resisted the temptation to peel out of the inn's sedate grounds as I returned to the police station. From one look at the Beer Belly Polka sitting smugly at the desk, I knew that word of Alie's antics was already spreading.

"Hey, Kotter, can you fix me up for a massage?" Cranshaw tweaked me.

"Negative, Sarge. But if you've got a hose, I can probably arrange for a mud bath."

"Kotter, you've got a bad attitude! You know that?"

I slammed into Randi's office. "This was supposed to be a plum assignment," I yelped.

Randi chuckled. "You ought to be careful what you wish for. Sometimes you get it."

"She's a brat."

Randi put a cool hand on the back of my neck and steered me toward the wall. I knew where we were going, and I didn't want to be there.

She put me in front of a photograph of a championship softball team. There I was, the shortest player, kneeling in the first row — the only one in this happy crew refusing to smile for the camera.

"You know a little something about brats, don't you?" Randi said.

"Yes, Captain."

The fight was draining from me. I looked at her, and she looked at me, both of us remembering.

* * * * *

I grew up in Hillsboro because both of my parents worked at the college. Mother was a physics professor. Father was the vice president of finance — which meant he had slightly less regard for people than an agent from the Internal Revenue Service. Children ranked even lower.

I was a grave disappointment to them. I was their only child, and they wanted a scholar, but there was something in me that did not love books. I was only happy outside. I loved the wild winds around me and the sky above, the grass and the dirt when they smelled of springtime, a rain so cold it left me shivering, and the dark night that made me feel invisible.

My parents and I simply did not get along. They were creatures of the earth, and I was of the air. They liked long and civilized evenings that began after dark, and I craved the mornings when the early sun created new, pastel colors every day. They thrived on measured conversations, and I preferred a churn of quick smiles, dancing eyes and a staccato of incautious words.

My father's name was Wendell Tyler Kotter. My mother's was Lynn Catherine Ives. They named me Wendy Lynn Kotter, as if I were the miniature personification of both.

They called me, formally, "Wendy Lynn" when they spoke to me, but they said I was free to use "Wendy" or "Lynn," whichever I preferred. They said it as though they were bestowing a great gift on me, but it was a phony academic freedom. They didn't want me to be me. They wanted me to be them.

Well, I didn't want to call myself Wendy because

it reminded me of him, and I didn't want to call myself Lynn because it reminded me of her. Fortunately I had one of those last names that everybody used anyway.

I liked being called "Kotter." It was a name *they* hadn't chosen, and it made me feel like myself.

By the time I reached the seventh grade, our household was in so much turmoil we could have used some United Nations peacekeepers. We had a huge fight over my extracurricular activities, and a truce was out of the question. They wanted me to be in the Reading Club at the Hillsboro Library. I wanted to play field hockey at school. They refused to sign the release form for sports. I skipped so many Reading Club meetings I was kicked out.

I stopped talking around the house or even meeting their eyes. They pinched their lips together disapprovingly and had long, low conversations with their colleagues in the psychology department.

I heard them talking one night when they thought I was asleep.

"What about therapy for her? Evelyn says there's a good child psychiatrist in Darby," Wendell said.

"She's just going through an adolescent phase, dear. Didn't you see her report card? Her grades are still good," Lynn said.

I wasn't bookish, but it didn't mean I was stupid. I kept my grades high enough to hold my parents at bay.

Funny, you never know where you'll find the path to salvation. I discovered it the summer after seventh grade by wandering into a sporting goods store. On the wall was a poster that showed Joan Benoit

23

Samuelson, the Olympic marathoner, running along a tree-lined rural road. She looked so peaceful I decided to try it.

There was a park in the middle of Hillsboro that served as a sort of class divide. On one side — our side — lived the families with the respectable jobs at the college and the hospital and the local businesses, the people who thought affluence was their birthright. On the other side were the paper mill workers and the employees and serving staff for our side, the people who had been Papa de Ville's world. The classes rarely met socially, but everybody used the park. I decided I would run there.

The morning after I saw the poster, I put on my cross-trainers from gym class and trotted along the uneven sidewalk until I got to the dirt running trails in the park. I followed a path to the ball fields, where I noticed a girls' softball team at practice. The players appeared to be high school age, and all but two of them were black. I didn't know anyone. Clearly they were not from my side of town.

The running trail circled the ball field, and I watched the practice as I went. At first I looked at the players, but after a while I was drawn to their coach — a slender and youthful African-American woman with a presence a Marine commandant would kill for.

She never stopped moving. She hit balls to the outfielders. She fixed someone's batting stance. She knocked an errant ball away before it hit her third base player in the head. She seemed to be aware of everything that was going on everywhere all the time, and her steady chatter kept her players focused.

Just being near her made me feel good. I circled

24

the field until the practice was over, and then I beat it.

I was back the next day. The day after that, I came by earlier and watched the coach as she hauled in the softball equipment and set up the bases for her practice.

I simply couldn't stay away. If I got tired running, I walked. Sometimes I quit altogether and just watched.

A week went by. Then the unexpected happened.

I got to the field as usual before the players arrived. I was circling behind the backstop near home plate when the coach looked right at me and said, "You."

I stopped dead. "Me?"

"What are you doing here?"

"Nothing. I — running. I'm not — I'm allowed to, aren't I?" I was scared to death.

"Do you like softball?"

"Uh, sure."

"Come on inside then."

I hesitated. "I don't know."

"You don't know?"

"No. I don't know."

I heard her chuckle for the first time in my life. It was the mirth of a fortune teller who knew more about you than you did and might tell you or might not. It was up to her, not you. "What's the matter?" she said. "Are you afraid you're the wrong color to come in here?"

It was exactly what I was afraid of. Once she said it, though, I didn't seem to mind anymore. I walked over to the gate and let myself in.

"What's your name?" she said.

I glanced down and kicked at the turf. "Wendy Lynn Kotter."

"What do people call you?"

How did she know to ask that? I was falling rapidly under her spell. "Kotter."

"Nice to meet you, Kotter. I'm Coach Wilkes. Do you want to play some catch?"

"Sure."

She picked a couple of gloves from a heap of them and tossed one to me.

"This is no good," I said.

"Why not?"

"I'm lefthanded." I pitched the glove back into the pile. It kicked against the other gloves as though it had been hit by gunshot and then lay still.

Why there was no thunder and lightning in the next moment I'll never know. Randie looked at me so piercingly I knew how Adam and Eve felt when they tasted the apple.

She walked toward me very slowly. I backed up until I was plastered against the fence. She didn't stop until she stood inches away from me, like a drill sergeant at boot camp. There was no one else around. I was terrified.

"Don't you ever show me disrespect," she said, her voice low and controlled. "Don't you ever show disrespect to the equipment. There was a civil way to do that, wasn't there?"

I nodded.

"I bet I can find a lefthanded glove, if you'd still like to play catch."

"I — yes, I would, Coach."

I never threw another piece of sports equipment

26

again. In the years to come, I never slammed down my batting helmet after I struck out. I never even kicked second base after I was caught stealing. When Randie Wilkes taught you a lesson, it took.

She tossed me a lefthanded glove, well-worn and grass-stained. I wriggled my hand into it reverently, as though it was a relic from the Hall of Fame. I wondered who had worn it before me and what sort of catches it had made. I smelled its leather smell and was happy. What was it about a glove that found the poetry in me?

Randie lobbed a throw, and I caught it snug in the pocket and threw it back smoothly. The next one came in a little harder, and pretty soon we had a nice rhythm going. Pitch and catch. Pitch and catch. The only sound that mattered was the *pop-pop-pop* of the ball cleanly hitting the leather.

Randie broke the silence as our game of catch went on. "What grade are you going into?"

I hesitated. I didn't want to talk about other troubling things. "Eighth."

"Do you like school?"

"It's okay."

"Do you have a favorite subject?"

"Not really."

"Are you on any sports teams?"

I put a little extra on the ball as I threw. "No."

Randie quit trying to draw me out. Obviously I was a more serious case than she first thought. A little while later, she glanced at her watch. "Listen, Kotter, I've got to set up for my practice. You want to help out?"

"Okay."

I helped her lug the water jugs from her car, a recent-model Jeep Cherokee, and I arranged the bats while she anchored the bases.

"This team is in the Police Softball League," Randie said. "It's for girls going into tenth, eleventh and twelfth grade. We play other teams in the county, and if we do well, we go to the state tournament at the end of the summer. I'm a corporal on the police force. I work in the community affairs division."

"I didn't know you were a cop."

"It's all right, Kotter. I haven't arrested anyone on the team all year."

I laughed. This coach was making me feel nervous and relaxed at the same time.

"You can stay and watch the practice if you want to," she said.

I wanted to. I retreated to the bench when the players started to arrive, sauntering and styling as athletes do. They greeted Randie warmly and went about their practice in that relaxed but alert manner of every good ballplayer.

I minded my own business until a batter smashed a foul ball off her shin. Randie was beside her almost before she hit the ground and hollered at me, "Kotter! Go to my car and get an ice pack out of the ice chest in the back!"

I scrambled off, elbows and knees pumping, not to mention my heart. Years later Randie teased me about it. "You looked like one of those skinny, little pale sandpipers with a hound dog after it. I never saw a child scurry so." All I knew at the time was that I was wanted.

I brought her the ice and made myself scarce

again. At the end of the practice, she asked me to wait until the players had departed. We walked to her car and she gave me one of the team's dark blue baseball caps.

"Here," she said. "I can use you again tomorrow."

I wore that cap everywhere, jammed down low over my eyes. My mother hated it but didn't ask me to get rid of it. Freedom of expression, you know.

I spent all of that summer hanging around with Randie's team and all of the next one, too.

At some point I wondered idly how a cop could have so much time for a softball team, but I never asked her. Little did I know it was a major part of her job. The police force knew what it was doing. It made the biggest drug bust in the history of Hillsboro after one of Randie's players whispered that some dealers from out of town were casing her neighborhood. Randie got a citation for that one.

The citation still hung on Randie's wall. I glanced at it, then looked back at her and shrugged. "I guess I can put up with Alie de Ville," I said.

Randie gave me that all-knowing chuckle. "Why don't you come to dinner tonight," she said. "Julie's barbecuing chicken and boiling up some corn on the cob."

"Thanks. I'll be there."

CHAPTER FOUR

Randie and Julie lived in a little house near the park on a street that served as a transition from one side of town to the other. They could have afforded better, but Randie didn't want to be too far from the meaner neighborhoods. Law enforcement was a full-time commitment for her.

Randie answered my knock. "Come on in. Dinner will be ready in a minute. Is that the beer?"

"Aye, aye, Captain," I said, lifting a paper bag in one hand and saluting mockingly with the other.

She kicked me in the seat of my pants as I

walked by. I could get away with sassing her in their house, but I always paid for it.

I went into the kitchen to put the beer in the refrigerator and see Julie.

"Kotter! How's it going?" Julie turned from the stove and melted against me in a sensuous hug. Randie watched amusedly from the doorway.

"Julie, let me take you away from all this," I said. "I'll show you sunsets in Paris, romance on the Riviera, candlelight cruises on —"

Julie shoved me away. "What's the matter, Kotter? Can't you get that clerk at the Rising Moon to pay any attention to you?" she teased.

"It's not the clerk that's the problem," Randie said. "It's that tennis pro."

Julie smiled mischievously. "What a pity. You should have seen her, Kotter. A body like that doesn't come along every day. Lean, muscular, skin like silk, lying there naked on my massage table. As soon as I touched her, she started moaning real softly, like she was fantasizing about —"

"Would you guys lay off?" I yelped.

"You started it," Julie said.

"She always does," Randie said drily.

I sighed. I wasn't going to win this one. "I think I could use a beer," I said.

"Not to mention a cold shower," Randie said. She got herself a beer, handed one to me and found Julie an Evian. Julie didn't drink. She said her body was a temple — which was perfectly obvious to anybody who looked. We sat down to eat.

"Julie," I said, "do you know what Alie de Ville did to me before you started the massage?"

"No, what?"

I explained how Alie had appeared in the anteroom. "That towel," I said. "A couple of millimeters lower, and I'd have been up close and personal with a pair of celebrity breasts."

"You know, Kotter," Julie said, "I haven't seen you this hot and bothered about a woman since Randie brought you here the first time."

"That was over the student teacher," Randie said, laughing.

"It was the worst," Julie said.

"No, it wasn't. It wasn't anywhere near as bad as when Kotter got involved with the pitcher at the state softball tournament," Randie said. She was laughing so hard she was dabbing her eyes with her napkin, and that got Julie laughing, too. I was blushing furiously.

"God, Kotter," Julie said, "didn't you ever learn to keep your hands to yourself?"

"Hey, it wasn't my fault! Both of those times they came on to me!"

"Kotter, I swear, I've caught crooks red-handed with better alibis than that," Randie needled.

"Do we really have to get into all this stuff?" I asked, still blushing.

"Yes, we do," Randie said. "It's good for you."

The summer after I finished ninth grade I was eligible to play on Randie's softball team, but I knew my parents would never let me. Wendell and Lynn still were holding out for the Hillsboro Library Reading Club.

I confessed my troubles to Randie about a week

before the softball season began. I didn't cry, but it was a close call.

Randie listened quite seriously, as though something important was in the balance, and maybe it was. "I think I can help," she said. "I'd like to pay a visit to your parents and do a little negotiating."

"They'll never change their minds."

"We'll see about that. But you have to promise me you'll do whatever we decide."

"I'm not going to that Reading Club."

Randie put her hands on my shoulders. "This isn't going to work if you don't trust me, and it isn't going to work if I can't count on you. Now what'll it be?"

I shifted uncomfortably. "Okay."

The next evening Randie came to our house. She arrived in a police cruiser and wore her uniform, all spit and polish with her hat pulled low — very intimidating. There were sergeant's stripes on her sleeves now. As she walked up the path over the expanse of lawn, I wondered what the neighbors were thinking. When people on our street encountered the law, they usually met with lawyers, not cops.

My parents were waiting, as gracious as they could be to someone not of their set. "You're very kind to take an interest in our daughter," my mother said.

"Not at all. It's been a pleasure knowing Wendy Lynn," Randie replied. I winced to hear her call me that, but she knew what she was doing. When in Rome, act patrician.

Wendell and Lynn ushered her into their study. I lounged on the living room couch, doing nothing. They talked for nearly an hour, and then Randie came out alone. I searched her face for clues, but she had been on too many witness stands to give anything away.

She sat on the couch beside me and set her hat on the coffee table. "Here's the deal," she said. "You can play softball, and you don't have to go to the Reading Club, but you do have to read. I'll be the one who chooses the books."

"What kind of books?" I asked warily.

Randie chuckled. "You'll know soon enough. Now come on, I'm taking you out for ice cream."

Randie never did tell me how she brought my parents around. Still, I wasn't the least bit surprised in the years to come when police departments around the state asked for her help in suicide and hostage situations. If she could persuade Wendell and Lynn, she could handle anything.

Randie kept her part of the bargain, making sure I did my reading. She gave me a variety of books — a biography of Arthur Ashe, *Huckleberry Finn,* a book of mythology, *The Longest Day* by Cornelius Ryan. To my astonishment, I liked them. I even read Ryan's story of D-Day twice. I still wasn't any scholar, but by the end of that summer, the printed word and I were getting along.

Mostly there was softball. A rookie in the major leagues couldn't have been any happier than I was. I wanted to play first base, but there was no way I was going to displace Amanda Jackson. She was in her second year on the squad, and she was awesome. Five foot ten and wreathed in muscle, Amanda went from first to third faster than anyone else on the team and led the league in home runs. With it all, she had the sunniest smile in the league, too.

I liked Amanda too much to resent her. I was content to play right field, instead. I batted second and developed a reputation as a pesky hitter.

We had a good team that year but not a great one, and we just missed the cut for the state tournament. The next year we were better and got to go.

That's what led to trouble.

I was fifteen and fast coming to the realization that prom nights did not make my heart go pitter-patter but pajama parties did. I accepted it without anguish, simply acknowledging it as something else that made me a perpetual outsider. I was used to not fitting in at home. I was comfortable being the only white kid on a team of African-American and Latin players. A long time ago I had figured out the only thing normal about me was if somebody took my temperature and it was ninety-eight point six.

The state tournament was held at Devon Academy, a boarding school about two hours away from Hillsboro. The teams stayed in the dormitories and ate together in the dining hall.

The buzz that year was all about a team from Maycomb County and its pitcher. Her name was Mary Margaret O'Day, but everyone called her Shamrock — for the obvious reason. She was going into her senior year, which put her a grade ahead of me.

Shamrock had set state records that summer for strikeouts and shutouts, and her team had gone undefeated. UCLA, one of the best softball schools in the country, had scouted her and was expected to offer her a scholarship.

Shamrock threw five pitches — fastball, change, rise, drop and curve — and every one of them was wicked. She was said to have joked she was sorry that batters got only three strikes, because it meant she couldn't use her whole repertoire.

The tournament schedule did not go our way. We were slated to start off against Maycomb County. Shamrock and her magic arm would be gunning for us.

"We could do worse," said Estelle Martinez, our shortstop. "We could be opening against the New York Yankees."

"When they had Babe Ruth and Lou Gehrig in the lineup," said Bonita Street, the left fielder.

When we filed into the dining hall for dinner on the eve of the tournament, we weren't any happier to discover we had been assigned the table next to Maycomb. They looked us over. We looked them over. They were big and they were burly, and they looked like the class act from a rugby tournament.

I spotted Shamrock, sitting in the middle of their table surrounded by her teammates, like the prize jewel she was. Unlike the rest of them, Shamrock was no bruiser. She was lean and rangy, her spare frame tucked into a green shirt and white jeans. She had no chest to speak of, and her hips were slim as a boy's. Her hair was short and dark, and there was an easy jauntiness to her.

If you had wanted to paint a picture of the luck of the Irish, you would have painted Shamrock. I couldn't take my eyes off her.

"Look at the size of them," Amanda, our first base player, whispered to me.

"I know."

"That one in the middle has got to be Shamrock."

"I noticed."

The Maycomb players saw us staring and took exception. "Hey," a player said. "What are you looking at?"

"Losers," I blurted.

The Maycomb team stiffened as one, as though they expected lightning to flash through the ceiling and strike me dead. Clearly no one had ever spoken to them that way.

Then Shamrock fixed me with a pitcher's eye. "You," she said. "Where do you bat in your lineup?"

"What's the matter? Don't you think you'll be able to pick me out from the rest of my team?" I shot back. It cracked up my teammates, pale as I was against them, and even got a quick snicker or two out of Maycomb.

Shamrock never wavered. "Where do you bat?" she repeated.

"Second."

"Well, I've got news for you. You're going down on strikes. You can put the 'K' on the scorecard now."

"The only one going down is you. I'll be hitting right back through the middle."

"Don't kid yourself," Shamrock said.

The two teams turned their backs on one another and huddled at their tables.

"Do you think you should have said all that?" asked Vanessa Chamberlain, our center fielder. "They're going to want to kill us now."

I shrugged.

"I can see it unfolding," moaned Estelle. "The first double-play ball I take covering second base, I get knocked to kingdom come."

"Sorry, guys. It just sort of happened," I said.

Amanda put an arm around my shoulders. "We know you can't help it, Kotter. We're with you."

The next morning we were pretty nervous as we congregated at the ball field. We watched Shamrock warming up. She looked like Nolan Ryan out there.

We batted first, with Estelle leading off. She struck out on three pitches, never taking the bat off her shoulder. I'm not even sure she opened her eyes.

Then it was my turn. I took a deep breath of the morning air and listened to the chirps and trills of the birds. I was damned if I was going to look nervous.

I settled in at the plate. Shamrock glared at me, then shifted into her windup. The pitch was the fastest I had ever seen in my life, and like Estelle before me, I never moved.

"Strike one!" the umpire bellowed. I was sure she was guessing. She couldn't have told any more about that pitch than I could.

Shamrock gave me a little smirk and set herself for the next delivery. It was another fastball, and I swung and missed. I managed to foul off the third pitch, but the one after that dropped down on me and I swung through it. I struck out — just as Shamrock had predicted.

She didn't even bother to look at me as I trudged back to the bench. I was furious. I hadn't even been a challenge for her. I had made the fatal mistake of worrying about her pitching instead of my hitting. I wasn't going to let it happen again.

Maycomb was leading 2–0 when I came up for my second at-bat in the fourth inning, but the score didn't reflect how bad it really was. Not one of us had reached base. Shamrock had a perfect game going.

She blew the first pitch by me, and I didn't even try for it. The second one was what I was praying for — a changeup I could handle. It came in a little bit low, but I went for it and did what I had vowed to do. I smoked it right back at the pitcher's mound.

It was a screamer of a line drive that could have done serious damage to a lesser athlete, but Shamrock miraculously got her glove in front of her face. The ball deflected straight up in the air, its venom draining, and she caught it easily on the way down. I was out.

I gave her a look as I trotted back to our bench, but she had her back turned — the coward. Still, I had settled the score. We were even.

Amanda gave me a pat on the back as I sat down. "That'll give her something to think about!" she said.

"Hell of a shot," Estelle said.

I nodded my thanks, feeling pretty good.

By the seventh and last inning, Shamrock was still rolling along on her perfect game, and we were trailing 4–0.

Estelle fanned for the third straight time, and then it was up to me.

We were desperate to make something happen. We didn't want to start the tournament with the humiliation of being on the wrong end of a perfect game. Losing was going to be bad enough.

"Get on base," Amanda whispered to me. "Just figure out some way to get on."

I took my place in the batter's box and eyeballed

Shamrock on the mound. I couldn't read the look in her eyes. She seemed far away, more contemplative than combustible, and I wondered if she wasn't in some sort of Zen state where pitchers go when they are two outs away from perfection.

I couldn't have been more wrong. Shamrock had something entirely different on her mind.

She reared back and threw, and the pitch came boring right at me, shoulder high, like a Scud missile. I had enough time to flinch away before it hit me, to take the knockdown that was intended to make me flop around and look foolish, but there was something in me that wouldn't let it happen.

Instead, I turned my back only a little bit and took the ball just under my right shoulder blade. I felt the welt rising immediately and the pain explode, but my only outward reaction was a short, sharp gasp that just the catcher could have heard.

I slammed down my bat and took a step toward Shamrock. She took one toward me. Before anything else could happen, though, Randie was beside me. She must have sprinted from the bench as soon as she saw the ball heading inside.

"Take your base, Kotter. Take your base," she said.

"It's okay, Coach. That's all I was going to do, anyway."

The umpire probably should have thumbed Shamrock out of the game, but she was as awestruck as everyone else. Randie didn't protest either. It wasn't her way. She believed in winning the game yourself, not with appeals to officials.

Anyway, Shamrock's perfect game was foiled. As I jogged down the line, my teammates stood and clapped, and I felt terrific. It's not every day you get applauded for being hit by a pitch.

After a moment, the Maycomb players gave Shamrock a hand too. She didn't acknowledge it. She just stood out there in whatever zone she was in and waited for the next batter. She still had two outs to go.

Vanessa Chamberlain, our center fielder, was next up. I took a long lead off first base. Now that the spell was broken, I intended to spoil Shamrock's shutout, too, if I could.

Vanessa had the same thing in mind. She swung at the first pitch and sent a nifty liner back up the middle. I took off at contact, only to see Shamrock spear the ball on the fly at her shoetops. I tried to scramble back to base, but my wheels spun under me on the dirt, and I went down at full extension. Shamrock calmly threw to first to double me off, and the game was over.

The Maycomb players shrieked and jumped and scampered onto the field for a celebration. They mobbed Shamrock. Even if she hadn't given them a perfect game, she had delivered a no-hitter. I got up slowly from the ground, brushed dirt off my uniform and tasted dust in my throat.

Maycomb finally settled down enough for the traditional, sportsmanlike team handshakes. I lined up at the end of my team and patted palms down the line, the way we were supposed to.

Shamrock was the last player on their side. I watched her coming, wondering what she would do. She did not pass by. Instead, she gave me a real handshake and said, "Hey, Kotter, can I buy you a Coke?"

I smiled in spite of myself. "Sure."

"OK. You know where the campus snack bar is — in that red brick building behind the dining hall? Put your gear away and meet me there in fifteen minutes."

My heart was pounding as I entered the snack bar. I was still in my dirt-stained uniform, but I had my cap tipped at a cocky angle, as though Hillsboro had won the game. The snack bar was closed for the summer, but there was a row of vending machines for the true snackaholics. It was cool and dark inside.

Shamrock was already there, waiting in the otherwise deserted building. She was still in her uniform, too. She dug change out of her pocket when she saw me and began dropping coins into the soda machine. They clanked loudly in the quiet, and the cans rolled noisily down the chute.

She handed me a Coke, and we popped the tops and sipped. I wondered whether she was feeling as awkward and nervous as I was.

"You really put it to us," I said. "That was a hell of a pitching performance."

"Well, you sure tried to put it to me, hitting that smash up the middle."

"I said I would, didn't I?"

"And I said I'd strike you out."

"Striking me out is one thing. I can't believe you threw at me. You gave up a perfect game to drill me."

"I thought you'd probably bail out."

"But you didn't know for sure."

"True. I thought about that. Then I figured I might have the chance for another perfect game someday, but I'd probably never pitch to you again. I had to go for it."

"You could have been tossed out of the game."

"I didn't care. Anyway," she shrugged, "every batter in this tournament is going to know what I did, and they'll all be thinking about it when they come up to the plate. I'm going to have an easy week."

I shook my head. "You're something else."

"Well, you're something else yourself."

By now I was trembling. Things were happening inside me that I'd never felt before. I knew I wanted this to go on, but I didn't know how to make it happen. All I could do was hope that Shamrock did.

"Listen, Kotter, you feel like going for a walk? There's a stream at the back of the school property and a little shady path beside it. It's real nice. You want me to show you?"

"Sure."

We took the walk. We had lunch together. We watched a couple of the other tournament games in the afternoon, sitting side by side and talking softball. It didn't exactly go unnoticed. By the time I joined my teammates for dinner, they were all over me.

"Kotter, what are you doing, fraternizing with the enemy?" Vanessa asked.

"How could you — after she deliberately threw at you?" Bonita demanded.

I shrugged. "She's a lot nicer off the field."

"We could be really mad at you," Estelle said, "except you're the one who broke up her perfect game."

43

"The hard way," Amanda added.

That was that. I continued to see Shamrock as the tournament went on. She kept mowing through the opposition, and eventually she pitched Maycomb to the championship. Meanwhile, the pressure was off us after losing that first game. We played solid ball the rest of the way and wound up coming in third. Randie was very proud of us and promised that next year, with Shamrock ineligible to play, we could win it all ourselves.

The night before the tournament ended, Shamrock stopped me after dinner. There were easy smiles between us now, but I thought I detected a little hesitation in her. "Hey, Kotter," she said, her voice too low for anyone else to hear, "meet me in ten minutes at the snack bar, okay?"

The building was as dark and cool and deserted as when we first met there. Shamrock lounged at the vending machines, her body slouched in the posture of a street tough. She gave me a cool once-over, and I felt my muscles tightening. There was something in this meeting that told me I would never be the same again.

I waited for her to speak. When she did, her voice was rough and husky, as though she didn't want to give anything away. "Kotter, it's been a great week. I'm going to miss you."

"Hell, Shamrock, I'm going to miss you too. It's been fun."

She shocked me by taking my hand. "We could — We could — You know what I mean?"

I wanted to answer her, but there was electricity shooting from her fingers into my palm and spreading everywhere, and I couldn't talk. The most I could do was twitch, so I twitched my hand until it squeezed hers back, and then somehow I managed to nod my head yes.

"These last few days, it's all I've been able to think about," she whispered.

"I — I've never done this before."

"It's all right. I have."

"A — a lot?"

"No, just once. At a softball camp last summer. With a college student who was umpiring."

"Where can we go?"

"We can't go to my room. My coach checks on us."

I thought a moment, then took the plunge. "We can go to my room. Coach Wilkes never checks on us."

"Okay. Let's go."

"No one should be around yet. It's too early. We should be able to sneak in without being seen."

No one bothered us as we walked to my dormitory. The tournament sponsors provided plenty of nighttime activities — movies, ping pong, video games, swimming, volleyball under the lights, music and nonstop snacks in the dining hall — and the dormitory was empty. We slipped into my room unnoticed. I wished briefly that the doors had locks on them, but I wasn't worried.

We sat on my bed. Shamrock took my hand, and I was embarrassed that my palm was sweaty.

"Are you scared?" she asked.

"Not scared exactly. Just — I don't know how to do anything."

"It's Okay. That's the way I felt last summer. Nature will take over, believe me." She kissed me softly on the cheek, and I felt my body start to hum in all the right places. She kissed me gently on the lips, and things weren't just humming anymore. Now it was a whole choir of angels belting away at the "Hallelujah Chorus."

So this was kissing. I marveled at how it could take a hard-nosed pitcher and turn her into enchantment and mystery. I tried to focus on the sensation of her lips against mine, but the rest of me kept getting in there, too. It was as much a part of these kisses as our mouths, crushing eagerly together.

I wrapped an arm around her middle. She pulled away and smiled and pressed my arm more tightly against her. "See?" she murmured. "I told you nature would tell you what to do."

Now as we kissed, we embraced, and in my mind I cursed the clothing that kept skin away from skin. I wanted nothing in between us, and at the same time I wanted this exquisite agony of desire to last forever. I wanted everything to hurry up, and I also wanted it to slow down so every single moment would be special. Romance had a way of making a mockery of time.

I was aware in a vague sort of way of activity in the hallway as my teammates filtered back to their rooms. I was much more focused on Shamrock's hand, which had crept under my shirt. Deft pitcher's fingers unhooked my bra and then lightly stroked my breasts. I prayed for her to find my nipples, but she was patiently exploring the curves and hollows of my chest, making me wait in sweet delirium.

"You're torturing me," I moaned, taking my hand and trying to push hers where I wanted it to go, but she resisted.

46

"It's your first time. It should last so you'll remember it," she said, and I gave in and let her lead at her own damnable pace.

Finally she got to my nipples. I thought they were the center of the universe — until Shamrock took advantage of my distraction to slip her tongue into my mouth. My body exploded into a kaleidoscope of pleasures. I squirmed and pressed against her and became infused with the holy truth that I would die if she didn't put her hand where it counted.

"Please, Shamrock, please," I begged, but she only laughed. Her hands lingered on my breasts and nipples, now taut and demanding.

Another millennium passed, and then Shamrock said, "Let's take our clothes off."

We did, discarding them in a heap on the floor. Shamrock looked at me approvingly, her eyes roaming boldly, until a puzzled look came into them. "What happened to your — Oh, shit. That's where I plunked you, isn't it?"

"Yeah."

She touched the ugly bruise gingerly and then kissed it with great care. "I can make it up to you," she promised.

I lay in the bed on my back, and Shamrock covered my body with hers, her skin slipping against mine in silken ecstasy. I raised my head and clutched her to me so I could use my mouth on her. I was crazed with the feel of her.

It was at that moment that the door to my room was thrust open. Randie stood there, taking in the whole scene.

She stiffened as surely as though she had been turned to stone. I desperately wanted to say

47

something on the order of, "Coach, this isn't what it looks like," but it is hard to say anything with another girl's breast in your mouth.

Anyway, it was exactly what it looked like.

Randie recovered quickly. She stepped into the room and closed the door behind her. Shamrock and I shrank away from each other and braced for God's wrath.

Randie's eyes looked at ours in the dim light, but she delicately avoided viewing the rest of our naked forms. "Shamrock, your coach was wondering where you had disappeared to. I'll tell her I've got you," Randie said. "Kotter, I'll see you in my room first thing in the morning."

That was all she said. She left.

"Oh, no, oh, no," I moaned. "We're done for. Shamrock, we've got to get you out of here."

The steel gaze of the pitcher was back in her eyes. "What for?"

"Huh?"

"She didn't throw me out. She didn't say anything, except she'd tell my coach I was here and she wants to see you in the morning."

"You mean you're thinking about staying?"

"I'm a pitcher. I like to finish what I start," Shamrock said playfully. She rubbed the side of my breast with the backs of her curled fingers, and I melted.

I was somewhat doubtful I'd be able to put the image of Coach Wilkes in the doorway out of my mind, but I found out you have very little concern for what's in your mind when a girl's fingers are touching you, tenderly stroking you, and she is whispering unrepeatable things in your ear, and you are bucking and sweating and shuddering like a lost soul flung to paradise.

Then Shamrock taught me to do what she had done, and we kept on doing it, just to make sure we got it right.

I rose early in the morning on the other side of innocence. Shamrock dressed and kissed me good-bye and went off to live her life. I showered and went to Randie's room with my hair still wet. I was feeling sheepish but otherwise unrepentant and surprisingly not very scared. Whatever she was going to do to me, I would accept.

Her door was open, so I walked in. Like any good cop, she already had managed to scrounge up a cup of coffee.

"Good morning, Coach," I said quietly.

"Have a seat on the bed, Kotter."

I sat. "Are you kicking me off the team?"

"No."

"Are you going to tell my parents?"

"No."

"Are you going to do anything to me?"

"Why should anything be done to you?"

"Because — because —" I started to cry uncontrollably. "Oh, God, Coach, because you trusted me and I let you down."

She did not let me cry alone. She came over and let me bawl in her arms until I finally sobbed myself out.

"How do you feel, Kotter?"

"I feel like I should just die."

"It's called 'remorse,' Kotter. Perhaps it's an emotion you will take care to avoid in the future. Now go and pack your things. The bus is leaving after breakfast."

CHAPTER FIVE

Julie cleared the dishes from the table. She never let Randie or me into the kitchen. She said we were hopeless in there.

Meanwhile, Randie got us a couple more beers. Julie said we both were competent enough to do that.

"Even after all these years," Randie said, chuckling, "I can't believe you were stupid enough to take Shamrock to your room. If I had thought you were in there, I never would have opened the door. I expected to find the place empty."

"Well, I never expected you to check on us. You *never* checked on us."

"I wasn't checking on you then. I was pretending to check on you, and only because Shamrock's coach was being a real pain about finding her. I had a pretty good idea what you two were doing, and I didn't want any part of it."

"And you didn't do anything to us, anyway."

Randie shook her head. "How could I? If word got out, it could have cost Shamrock that UCLA scholarship she was in line for. It certainly would have turned the state tournament into a major scandal." Randie hollered into the kitchen, "Did you hear that, Julie? Do you see what I was up against? That's why the day Kotter lost her virginity was absolutely the worst."

Julie stuck her head out of the kitchen. "Typical. Kotter gets laid, Randie, and you get screwed."

"Hey, it wasn't any picnic for me, either," I protested. "Listen, Randie, I didn't care whether Shamrock respected me in the morning, but I sure as hell cared whether you did."

"You expect me to buy that?" Randie asked, and the look in her eyes told me I was in for it. "Now tell me the truth, Kotter. What do you remember most — being in the sack with Shamrock or being miserable with me afterwards?"

"That is an unfair question. It's been years, and everything worked out all right."

Randie got out of her chair and stood looming over me, as though I was one of her police recruits — and not a very good one, at that. She launched into a very humorous distortion of my Miranda rights. "Tell the truth, Kotter. You have no right to remain silent. Anything you don't say will be held against you. There is no lawyer in the land who will dare to take your case. If you do choose to remain silent, every single one of your constitutional rights will be violated, and I will personally beat the shit out of you. Now talk!"

"All right, all right. What can I say? It was a great first lay."

Randie sighed. "You got away with murder."

I smiled. Now it was my turn to needle her. "Hell, Randie, if I knew then what I know now, I wouldn't even have been worried when you walked in on us."

"What do you mean by that?"

"Back in those days, I thought you were just a red-blooded, All-American coach with your eyes on the guys. I had no idea you had any sort of appreciation for what I was doing. I didn't know about you and Julie."

"No, that had to wait until your next sexual escapade."

I winced. "Are we going to go into that, too?"

Randie was maddeningly serene. "You bet we are."

The summer after my encounter with Shamrock, Randie's prediction came true. Our softball team won the state championship and I was one of the players the team counted on.

As I entered my senior year at Hillsboro High School, I should have been feeling pretty good about myself; but I knew better. Instead, I was aware of being headed for one of those crises that mark your life forever, and naturally it had to do with my parents. Wendell and Lynn were assuming I would go to some small, egghead college — Hillsboro would be nice but not mandatory — for liberal arts, to be followed by graduate school. Well, I didn't want to go to any stifling, antiseptic ivory tower. I wanted to be a cop.

I put off the confrontation as long as possible by letting Wendell and Lynn think I was conforming. I enrolled in academic courses, took my SATs and even sent away for some college catalogues.

Meanwhile, Randie had made lieutenant, faster than anyone in the history of the department. As a sidelight she started an introductory program in criminal justice for high school seniors, and I signed up, of course. There were ten of us, meeting after school at the Hillsboro police station. I loved hanging around there, usually showing up early and staying late. Randie and the other cops encouraged me and included me as much as they could, whether it was inventorying the evidence locker or simply photocopying their reports when they were too pressed to do it themselves.

I learned a lot about police work — about the diligence and patience in the face of constant stress, long stretches of boredom and an endless parade of human suffering. I learned about the wisecracking that hid the hearts behind it, the lousy hours, the camaraderie of the force and the lethal joy of stalking crooks. The more I learned, the more I wanted to stay.

My school work was going fairly well — because it had to. I knew if my grades fell, Wendell and Lynn would yank me out of the police station faster than you could say "Hamlet, Prince of Denmark."

I probably could have kept out of trouble until the spring — except for the arrival of the student teacher.

Her name was Deb Jaworski, and she was a physical education major at Hillsboro College. She showed up in late October in my first period gym class.

Deb Jaworski was as fearsome an athlete as ever set foot on a playing field. She was big and strong and not very fast, but she had the reflexes of a cobra.

In the fall she played goalie on the college hockey team, where she was heard to say, only half-humorously, "Why run up and down the field when you can stand in the goal cage and be a hero?"

In the winter she played volleyball and was the heart of the squad; but it was in the spring she really excelled. That was the season she played softball.

She was a catcher and an All-American, but she was known in local sports lore mostly as the only woman ever to hit a ball out of the Hillsboro College stadium. It was such an extraordinary feat that a plaque was mounted at the top of the center field bleachers to mark where the ball passed overhead, still rising as it did.

Her teammates called her "Jaws," and so did the grateful headline writers for the sports pages. It fit much better than "Jaworski." When she arrived in gym class, she allowed that we could call her "Miss Jaws."

Jaws would have been welcomed by our class under any circumstances; but as it was, we regarded her with nothing short of relief. Gym class was otherwise the iron province of Mrs. Engler, a stern tyrant so ancient we swore she began teaching when bloomers were still risqué. Her first name was Diane, which the other teachers shortened to "Di" when they talked to her. Her students embraced the sound of it. There wasn't one of us who hadn't muttered, "Die, Engler."

Jaws endeared herself to us during her very first class. While Mrs. Engler was threatening to flunk anyone who didn't begin the week with ironed gym clothes, Jaws gave us a wink.

It was all I needed to develop a mad crush on her. I never could resist jocks, anyway.

Jaws was fun. She freed us from Mrs. Engler's regimen of calisthenics and let us play soccer and flag football and other reckless games. Anyone who didn't try hard was ordered to run laps. Anyone who gave her a hard time had to run them, too.

Gym class changed from drudgery to joy. Then came the day when matters got a little out of hand.

A bunch of us were in the locker room early before class. Linda Franzione, who played on the field hockey team, was showing us a doll she bought at the school store. It was dressed in a miniature hockey uniform, including a kilt in the school colors just like Mrs. Engler always wore. Beth DeWitt got the bright idea to get some cotton out of the first aid kit on the wall and give the doll white hair, just like Mrs. Engler's. Estelle Martinez, my pal from softball, had a pin cushion with some straight pins for her home economics class, and one thing led to another until I was stabbing pins into the Engler doll, voodoo style.

"Die, Engler!" I said and stabbed. "Die, Engler! Die, Engler!"

It was all very funny. My friends were laughing and squealing and encouraging me, and then suddenly they weren't. In the deathlike silence I looked up to see Jaws standing there.

There was no denying what we were doing. We were shark chum.

Jaws was calm. "May I have that, please?" she said, holding out her hand for the doll. I gave it to her, pins and all. Already I regarded it as *the evidence*.

"I think you girls better get out there and run some laps," Jaws said, "and don't stop until I come to get you."

Laps were not a very bad punishment. I was feeling grateful and relieved as I headed out. Then I heard Jaws say, "Not you, Kotter. You stay here."

I stopped dead. My friends rushed for the door in a shameless display of self-interest, desperate to get out before Jaws called anyone else back. I was going to walk this plank alone.

"I take it you're the ringleader here," Jaws said.

I shrugged. I wasn't really, but I wasn't going to rat out anyone else, either. It was the code we lived by.

"There are a couple of things we can do with you," Jaws said matter-of-factly. "The most logical would be to tell Mrs. Engler about this and let her handle it. How does that sound to you?"

It sounded terrible. No doubt it meant Mrs. Engler would flunk me, and although my parents weren't very big on gym, a failing mark in any subject certainly wouldn't look good on my transcript. The jig would be up.

I swallowed. "Did you say you might have something else in mind?"

"Possibly. You could stay after school and deal directly with me."

I hesitated. If I stayed, I would miss Randie's criminal justice session, and she would want to know why. "I'm supposed to be at the police station," I said, "for a special program."

"Fine with me. We can just turn this whole matter over to Mrs. Engler."

"No, wait. I'll come after school."

"All right. Meet me here. Wear your gym clothes."

"What will I have to do?"

"You'll see."

I wasn't happy, but it was clearly the best deal I was going to get. I went to the pay phone and called the police station. I left a message with the Beer Belly Polka, already beginning his terminal duty as desk sergeant, to tell Randie I had an assignment at school and couldn't make her program. I didn't have the nerve to talk to her myself.

Then I sweated out the rest of the day until I reported back to Jaws. She gave me a businesslike nod, a sort of teacher's equivalent to the preacher who loves the sinner but hates the sin.

"Come with me," she said, and I followed her outside. It was a fine fall afternoon, just at the end of the sun's warmth but before the evening chill set in. I was comfortable in my gym shorts and T-shirt, but if Jaws kept me too long, I would be wishing for my sweatshirt.

She led me down to the football field, where the school district had just erected tall, concrete bleachers on the home side. "Let's see you run to the top and back down," she said.

I was in pretty good shape. I did it, and it wasn't too bad.

Jaws had clicked a stopwatch when I started. She eyed it critically and said, "I think you can do that faster. Try it again."

I pushed myself and felt it, but not enough to let on. Jaws read the stopwatch with disdain. "Once more," she said.

I gave her a look, the student's patented mix of disgust and defiance. Jaws did not let it pass. "Anytime you want to stop," she said, "we can go and talk to Mrs. Engler about what you did."

I headed for the bleachers and went all out. By the time I was finished, I was soaked with sweat, my chest was heaving and my leg muscles were burning. Jaws checked that damned stopwatch. "You're getting there," she said. "Do it faster and maybe I'll let you go."

There was no way I had the energy for it. "Come on, Miss Jaws, isn't this enough?"

"Kotter, I'm surprised. You're not crying uncle already, are you?"

That made me mad. I turned to the bleachers again, but my left calf cramped, and I crumpled like a bird with a bad wing. Instantly Jaws knelt on the ground and worked on my screaming muscles. She knew what she was doing, and after some bad moments, the pain drained away.

I was left with the sensation of her touch — a soothing combination of strength and tenderness. I realized with the stark self-awareness of Eve after the apple that I wanted more of it.

I looked at Jaws and found her looking at me. It came to me how I must have appeared as she unknotted the cramp — my face strained and body arched, as though her magical hands were not on my leg but elsewhere.

I should have turned away from her, but I did not. She was a student teacher, and she certainly should have turned away from me, but she did not.

"If you want more out of me, it's up to you," I said, my voice a little unsteady. "I can't do any more. You can tell Engler or do whatever."

"That's 'Mrs. Engler' to you, and you know it."

"Are you going to tell her that, too?" I knew I should shut up and stop pushing her, but I couldn't seem to help myself, lying there exposed and vulnerable. I wanted a reaction from her, one way or the other.

I was shivering now, mostly because I was cooling down but also because of the emotions bubbling within. Jaws stood up and said, "Let's get you inside before this chill makes you cramp again."

She extended her hand, and I grasped it to pull myself off the grass, then deliberately swayed against her, attracted by the muscular solidarity there. She righted me with a rough touch that lingered longer than it should have.

I was done in and limped slightly as we returned to the gym. No one else was there. The varsity football players were still out on the practice field, and the rest of the fall sports teams had away games. Jaws took out her keys, unlocked the towel room and gestured for me to go inside with her. She locked the door behind us.

The walls were lined with shelves and shelves of coarse white gym towels, notorious for being too skimpy to cover the tall girls from chest to crotch. I didn't have that problem, but I knew Jaws would, and the image caught in my mind.

In my exhaustion I leaned against the door. Jaws put her hands on my shoulders, pinning me there. "What do you want?" she said.

I should have said, "A towel," and that would have been that, but I didn't. "You know what I want."

"Tell me."

"God damn it!"

"Tell me."

"Just do it."

She leaned in and kissed me. I closed my eyes and lost myself in the raw sensuality and power of an athlete who believed the human body was put on this earth to perform.

This was even more forbidden than being with Shamrock, and I couldn't believe how much it was turning me on.

Jaws slipped her hand under my T-shirt and felt my breasts through the thin fabric of my sports bra. I started to melt against her, but she pulled back abruptly, shoved me against the door and held me there. "You tramp," she said, but it was with a forgiving lilt in her voice, "you've done this before, haven't you?"

"Just once, I swear. Two summers ago at the state softball tournament. Come on, kiss me again."

"You're desperate for it, aren't you?"

"Please, you're torturing me."

Her lips took me back to delirium, and her hands created new excitement under my shirt. I felt for her hips but didn't have the nerve to explore further. Anyway, what I really wanted was what she was doing to me.

She yanked down my gym shorts and panties, turning them into shackles around my ankles. I was crazed with desire but also with fear — who else had a key to the towel room door?

Jaws didn't give me much time to wonder. Her fingers went where it counted, touching, teasing, stroking, now gentle, now demanding, making me care about nothing in the universe except what was happening here, here, here. She knew what she was doing, and I was eager and inexperienced and overwhelmed, and in no time at all I was clinging to her to keep myself upright while wave after rapturous wave pounded through me in violent release.

"Holy hell!" I gasped and collapsed against her. She held me, but it wasn't in tenderness so much as physical support. If I thought my muscles were in disarray coming into the towel room, they were demolished now.

Jaws kissed me on the forehead. "We better get out of here."

"But what about you?"

"Another time. Football practice should be over any minute."

I collected myself shakily. Jaws waited while I showered. I was still pretty dazed when I reappeared, and she seemed quite pleased with what she had done. "I may have to keep you after school again tomorrow," she said.

I was torn between duty and desire. "If I don't show up at the police station, I'm going to be in big trouble. I'm probably already in big trouble."

She gave me one very smoldering look, and I gave in. "All right. Suppose I meet you as soon as my last class ends? We can be together a little bit, and then I'll go over there."

"Sounds good to me, darlin'."

I didn't sleep that night. I had never been so fevered in my whole life. I kept thinking about being with her and how much I wanted it again and again and again.

Getting through the school day was a torment, especially gym class. While we changed out of our school clothes, my friends ragged on me about getting caught with the Engler doll, and I had to pretend to be miffed at Jaws.

"Thanks to you, I lost ten bucks on that doll," Linda Franzione said.

"You got off easy. I'm the one that had to take the rap for the whole thing," I said.

"Poor Kotter. All you had to do was stay after school a little bit," Beth DeWitt said.

"Hey, she damn near killed me out there."

"At least she didn't tell Mrs. Engler," Estelle said.

We went into the gym. Jaws was there, of course, and my body started to quiver. I made a show of ignoring her. Fortunately everyone assumed my coolness was petulance, not a desperate bridle on some rather intense cravings.

Jaws was having none of it, though. As she assigned us to teams for flag football, she stood right behind me and put her hands on my shoulders, taunting and tantalizing me, as she knew it would. I blushed and looked down and tried to figure out a way to breathe. My classmates snickered. Thank heavens they didn't know the real reason why Jaws was singling me out.

My classes passed in agonizing slowness. If there had been any tests, I would have flunked them. I simply couldn't concentrate on school work.

At the last bell I flew back to the gym. Jaws gave me a beckoning smile, her eyes dancing in welcome, but I was seething. "How could you do that to me in class today?" I demanded. "Why didn't you just come over and start undressing me?"

"Are you that hot for it?" she teased.

"I can't hide what I'm feeling. I'll give it away."

"Kotter, you're already giving it away."

I groaned in disgust. Jaws laughed, and after a moment, I laughed, too. "Come on," she said. "The towel room waits."

Not for us, it didn't. The laundry service workers were in there, restocking the towels.

"Damn," Jaws muttered.

I was disappointed but also relieved. "I can't stay. I've got to get to the police station."

"Listen, I have a hockey game tomorrow afternoon. Can you get there?"

"I think so. I'll stop by after my police course. I might miss the first period, but I'll be there."

I took my time going to the station, which was only a few blocks from the high school. I didn't want to arrive much before Randie started the class. She glanced at me when I slipped into a seat, but she didn't say anything. I wondered wildly whether I might get away with my absence yesterday and grew positively giddy as she dismissed us. I stood up quickly, only to hear, "Kotter, could I see you for a moment?"

I hauled myself to the front of the room and gave her a winning look, which was all the defense I had. Randie was not charmed.

"Well?" she said.

How could such a simple word unnerve me? I blushed deeply and was grateful the Engler doll episode was silly enough for me to be embarrassed, because I had no intention of telling the truth, the whole truth and nothing but the truth. Humbly I confessed to the doll and to being kept after school.

Randie was unforgiving. "I expect better from you. I'm fining you a twenty-dollar donation to the Police Softball League."

I winced. As Randie knew, I was saving my allowance to go with some friends to a Melissa Etheridge concert next month in Willington, about an hour's drive from Hillsboro. We were planning to make a day of it, so I needed money for my ticket, gas and dinner. I also had an eye on a new vest for the occasion.

"Come on, Lieutenant, I already had to stay after school. Isn't this double jeopardy?"

"We'll make it a forty-dollar donation, and since you brought it up, I'd like an essay from you on 'double jeopardy.' Any more questions?"

"No, ma'am." I exhaled deeply. Considering what I had really done, I was still getting off easy.

My routine changed. I saw Jaws at every opportunity, although it was difficult to get time alone. She had a place on campus, but she shared it with two roommates and someone always seemed to be around. Sometimes we met in the towel room, but we were afraid of being seen together around school too often. Sometimes Jaws picked me up in her car, and we'd head for a secluded spot. I knew where the police patrolled, so we were fairly safe from detection, but the accommodations weren't exactly luxurious. No matter what we did, we always seemed to be hurried and fumbling. We were living in a perpetual state of frustration, which was titillating but not very satisfying.

Meanwhile, I wasn't hanging around the police station as much. I went to Randie's classes but I quit arriving early or staying late. Some days I scarcely looked up from my notebook. I just sat there trapped in a sexual haze.

Randie let one week pass, but not two. She waited by the door after she dismissed us, and as I walked by, the last to leave, she collared me. "You and I are going to have a talk," she said.

I assumed she would take me to her office, but she steered me toward the back of the station until I realized in panic where we were going. We were on our way to the interview room where the cops interrogated their suspects. It was known as "The Rathole," because the idea was to get the suspects to rat, and what went on in there was called "The Confession Session." Randie must have broken down a million people in there. I wanted no part of it.

She took me inside. The Rathole was a sad-sack, barren place, furnished with one long wooden table and a couple of chairs. The lighting cast an uncomfortable glare, and the sallow wallpaper had been fading for years, deliberately neglected. The room looked like a bad movie set, which was exactly what it was supposed to look like. It could work wonders on a guilty conscience.

Randie pulled the curtains across the two-way mirror that separated The Rathole from the observation room behind it. She turned off the microphone that normally let someone in the observation room listen in. We were cut off. Anything that happened in there was going to happen without witnesses.

"Sit down," she said, and I sat. She leaned against the table and gave me a piercing look. "Now what the fuck is going on?"

I had never heard her use an obscenity before. It seemed so violent, she might as well have hit me.

"Noth —"

"And don't give me any of your 'nothing' shit."

"Okay, okay. Just give me a minute."

Randie came over and put her hands on the chair's arms, penning me in. "You don't have that option. Spill it. Now."

I spilled. Not only did I spill, but I gushed and I groveled. Once I got started, it was a torrent of words, and every single one of them was self-incriminating. No one could wipe the Fifth Amendment out of the Constitution as cleanly as Randie could.

I didn't want to stop talking, because I didn't know what would come next, but eventually I had to. For a while there was silence. Randie appeared to be thinking, but she did not seem upset. Her voice was mild when she spoke.

"We can't have this," she said. "You should have come to me, but I guess you didn't know that."

"You mean I'm not in trouble?"

"Not with me."

She went to the telephone, mounted on the wall by the observation room mirror, and asked the Beer Belly Polka for an outside line. In horror I watched her punch in my home number. I wanted to bolt, but there was no place to go. Randie was the only person I had ever run to.

My mother must have answered the phone because Randie said, "Hello, Dr. Ives. This is Lieutenant Wilkes at the police station... No, everything's fine. When there's something wrong, we come to the door, like the Marines... If you don't mind, I've asked Wendy Lynn to stay and help me out this evening. I hope you're not having her favorite meal... Oh, she tends to skip dinner? Well, I'll make sure she eats. I'll bring her home myself, so you don't have to worry. Bye-bye."

Randie punched in another phone number, one I didn't know. "Hey, you," she said, a tenderness in her voice I had never heard before, "I'm heading out now. I've got Kotter with me. See you in a few."

She hung up and turned to me. "Come on, Kotter, let's get going."

"Where are you taking me?"

"To my world."

I was confused, but I shut up. I didn't imagine anything bad could happen to me in Randie's world.

We went to her car, a later model of a Jeep Cherokee than the one she owned when I met her, and she drove toward the park, stopping in front of the modest house I would come to know so well.

"Is this yours, Lieutenant?"

"Yes, but I share it."

I didn't know what I would find inside — a

68

boyfriend, kids, elderly parent — but I certainly didn't expect a goddess. There stood Julie, upright and towering, in a flowing shift of vibrant red, black and green, the colors of her African heritage, its vertical stripes making her look even taller.

Randie, still looking spiffy in her police uniform, kissed this angelic creature and took her hand. She looked at me, and she nodded yes to the question roaring in my head.

I felt cold and warm at the same time. I felt disoriented, but I also felt more centered than ever before. I knew that for the rest of my life, I had a place to come to. Randie had taken me in. Once she had found a lonely kid and made her a part of a team, and now she was showing me there were other people like me and it was all right.

I swayed at the force of it, and Randie came over and gripped me as though I might fall. "Are you okay?" she asked.

"I just didn't expect this."

"Do you want to leave?"

"No, no! That's the last thing I want."

Then Julie spoke. Her voice was untroubled, as flowing as the shift she wore, as though it rose from a deep and peaceful place within. "Goodness, Randie, what have you done to this child? She's as scared as a trapped rabbit."

"I did scare her. She needed to be scared. It wasn't the first time, and it won't be the last."

"Well, she doesn't need to be scared now. She needs to feel welcome." Julie came over and grasped both of my hands in hers, and I found myself relaxing in spite of myself. She had the hands of a healer, gentle and soothing and giving. I didn't know then what she did for a living, but I knew whatever it was, it involved helping others. "Kotter, I'm Julie. Although you didn't know about me, you've been a part of my life for a long time. Randie is always talking about you. I'm so pleased you're finally here. Now can I get you something? Soda or juice?"

"Just some water would be fine, ma'am. Thank you."

Julie gave Randie a long look of mocking sorrow. "Has Randie been filling you up with that militaristic crap? You don't have to say 'ma'am' to me. 'Julie' is fine."

She went into the kitchen and returned with some Evian in a glass that had the seal of the Hillsboro Police Department etched in it. I was thirsty. It had been a trying afternoon.

"Well, Julie," Randie said, "we found out why Kotter has made herself so scarce of late."

"Why is it?"

"It seems she was seduced by that student teacher."

"The one who made her stay after school?"

"The very same."

Randie and Julie regarded me speculatively, much the way a jury eyes the prisoner in the dock, gauging whether she is capable of committing the crimes of which she is accused. I shrugged. Guilty is as guilty does.

"Girls will be girls," Julie said and laughed. I heard the liberating chimes of heaven in that laughter and felt saved. I was becoming more captivated with her by the minute.

Randie came up behind me and wrapped her arms around me, cradling me against her. I was getting more affection in this room than I'd had in a lifetime.

"What do you think we should do to you, Kotter?" Randie asked.

"I don't care. Do whatever you want. Just let me stay here forever."

"Personally, I think we should feed her," Julie said. "It's just spaghetti, Kotter. Is that okay?"

"You bet," I said.

"Just spaghetti" turned out to be homemade pasta and tomato sauce from scratch. Julie enjoyed cooking. More precisely, she enjoyed cooking for others. We kept talking as she got the meal ready and sat down to eat.

"The problem with Kotter being seduced by the student teacher," Randie said, mortifying me, "is that they are doing it in public places."

"Oh dear. That won't do," Julie said.

"No, it won't. I suppose we're going to have to bring the student teacher here, too. I'm inclined to drive to her place, cuff her and put her in the back seat of a patrol car, but it might be counter-productive. What do you think, Julie?"

"Undoubtedly it would be. The rapport will probably be better if Kotter just invites her."

They were toying with me. There was nothing to be done but sit and take it. Life would be full of these moments.

By the end of the evening, I had agreed to bring Jaws to their house, although I was as nervous about it as any girl taking her date home for the first time.

If I was fidgety, Jaws was positively stricken when I told her about it. "I don't care if she is your friend. She's a cop! Student teachers go to jail for molesting students, or haven't you heard?"

"You only go to jail if you don't cooperate," I said. In a perverse way, I was starting to enjoy this. Randie's intervention had given me the upper hand in a relationship that otherwise had gone almost exclu- sively Jaws' way. "Consider yourself blackmailed."

The next evening was Friday — no police class. It was dark and cool, with a wild wind rattling the brittle autumn leaves. I slipped out of the house without telling Wendell and Lynn where I was going. They had a dinner party at the college president's house, one of those command performances, and wouldn't be able to do anything except get exasperated when they discovered my absence.

I jammed my Police Softball League champions' cap down against the wind and stuck my hands into my jeans pockets. I kept thinking about what I was doing. I was going to meet my girl, I was taking her over to Randie's house, and society be damned. I didn't feel like a kid anymore.

Jaws and I had arranged to meet in the Hillsboro Library parking lot. Nobody we knew would even think to go to the library on a Friday night.

Jaws drove a dark green Mustang convertible with so much power it practically needed clearance from Mission Control. Everything about it was brazenly erotic, its lean, sleek chassis and leering grillwork, supple leather seats and haughty tinted glass. I loved that car.

Jaws was parked in the shadows, the motor running against the evening chill. I slipped into the passenger's seat. Normally she did something obscene to me as soon as I got close enough, but not tonight. I gave her a look. The warmup suit and cross-trainer shoes she favored were replaced by khaki slacks, loafers, a turtleneck shirt and tasteful V-neck sweater.

"Christ! Where are you going? To a job interview?"

"What about you? You look like an undercover cop."

"Is that supposed to be an insult?"

"Oh for God's sake, just give me directions to where we're going."

Jaws was nervous, all right. She drove to the house without speaking. Julie let us in, greeting me with a hug and Jaws with a warm handshake. "Randie's on her way," Julie said. "Kotter, why don't you get a couple of Cokes out of the refrigerator and make yourselves at home? I'm in the middle of stroganoff."

We had barely popped the tops on our sodas when we heard Randie's Jeep Cherokee pull into the driveway. Jaws' shoulders tightened. Then they tightened some more as Randie entered. She was in uniform. The mirror-bright hat brim, the spit-shined shoes and the gold lieutenant's bars on her collar gave her a look of blue steel.

It had its effect on Jaws. She had that sweaty glaze that comes when all you can think about is calling your lawyer.

Randie's eyes did a slow scan of Jaws, taking in the broad shoulders and the big hands and the athlete's build that no clothes could civilize. Randie's search was so thorough, she should have had a warrant.

"Hey, Lieutenant," I said. "This is Jaws."

"Kotter, considering the circumstances, you might as well call me 'Randie' when you're in the house."

That sure surprised me. Someday I would figure Randie out, but now was not the time. The last thing I expected from her was this Officer Friendly routine.

Jaws was disarmed. Her natural cockiness returned, and she smiled at Randie. Personally, I thought it was a little premature to be feeling comfortable, and I decided to keep my mouth shut as much as I possibly could. After all, I hadn't even gotten through the introductions without being thrown for a loop.

"Have a seat, you guys," Randie said.

Jaws and I sat on the sofa at a polite courting distance. We didn't touch.

Randie and Jaws had a lot of mutual friends through Randie's involvement with the Police Softball League and Jaws' college softball team. They had a very pleasant conversation going until Randie paused, suddenly thoughtful, and said, "So tell me, Jaws, whatever were you thinking when you took a high school student into the towel room and sexually exploited her?"

Jaws gasped. She turned so stone still, she forgot to breathe. Randie got up and stood in front of her.

"Well?" Randie demanded.

"I — it — it was mutual," Jaws croaked.

"Mutual? It's mutual when you find a kid fooling around with her friends and turn it into such a big deal that she fears for her academic standing, her future and her family life if she doesn't do exactly what you say? It's mutual when you order her into her gym clothes and lock her in a room where you have an absolute hold over her? Is that what you call mutual?"

"Oh my God," Jaws said hoarsely.

"You can tell the school district it was mutual. You can tell your college adviser it was mutual. You can tell Kotter's parents it was mutual."

"Lieutenant, please don't do this. I'll do anything you say. I swear to God I'll never touch her again."

Randie chuckled. "No need. Fortunately for you, Jaws, it *was* mutual," she said mildly. "Come here, Kotter." She put me in front of her, both of us facing Jaws, and wrapped her arms around me protectively. "Kotter's the baddest kid I know, but she's going to be a good cop, and I'm not going to let anything interfere with that. So listen up, Jaws. Kotter has got to spend more time at the station again, and you two have got to stop doing it in public places. Understood?"

"Yes, Lieutenant."

Randie's infernal chuckle came again. "I thought you all were going to call me Randie."

"The problem is, you keep acting like a lieutenant," I said, which was a very brave thing to do, considering that Randie had me folded against her. All she did, though, was give me an affectionate squeeze. I wasn't the villain tonight.

Julie was waiting patiently to serve dinner, so we moved our discussion to the table. She had prepared her usual masterpiece — the stroganoff and a vegetable medley and some homemade bread that came from the oven, not from one of those tinker-toy breadmakers.

"After we finish dinner, Julie and I are taking

you two out," Randie said. "Have you ever heard of the Hollies?"

We hadn't. Randie smiled and explained. It was a discreet retreat snuggled into the foothills out past the Buena Vista Country Club. If you didn't know where it was, you'd never find it.

A discerning clientele liked it that way. Patrons could escape to its finely furnished rooms, small gourmet restaurant, bar with walk-in fireplace, mountain trails and nightly live music that was always soft, urgent and throbbing. Its official name was the Forest House, but it was universally called by its nickname because the two women who owned it both were named Holly. Fortunately one was tall and one was short, so they were known as Big Holly and Little Holly.

After dinner, Jaws and I helped Julie clean up, while Randie changed out of her uniform. She came back looking really slinky in a clingy black shirt and slacks, and Julie slipped into the bedroom with her before they said they were ready to go.

Randie drove us out there. The evening had gotten even colder. The heater was going full blast, but the Jeep window beside me still felt like ice. I looked outside. Bold constellations were the only light, burning above the silhouettes of pine trees bending and shaking in the wind. It was so dark and peaceful and perfect, sitting there in the back of the Jeep, with Randie and Julie in the front and Jaws next to me primly holding my hand. I wouldn't have cared if some omnipotent presence had reached down and sealed us for all eternity in that moment in time.

There was no landmark for the Hollies, only an inconspicuous break in a low stone wall. I had passed by countless times without knowing what it was. Randie turned in, the gravel lane crunching under her tires. We followed the drive as it twisted through a thick grove of pines until we came to a clearing where the tidy brick inn was situated, its first story windows lit charmingly by single candles like something out of colonial times. Outside the Jeep, snatches of music were blown to us on the wind.

The Hollies were doing a business that Friday night. The parking lot was filled, mostly by cars with local license plates that had come for the evening, but also by some with out-of-state plates there for the weekend.

Randie put an arm around me and walked me toward the door, leaving Julie to take care of Jaws. "Whatever you see here stays here," she said. "Okay?"

I nodded, quite curious now. As soon as we entered, shrugging off the chill, I understood why. I saw a couple of teachers from school at a table for two, leaning toward each other so closely their breasts nearly touched. I saw a softball coach from the team we beat in the semifinals melted against another woman in a slow dance, and if I wasn't mistaken, I saw a U.S. senator, who must have arrived in that Mercedes in the parking lot with the out-of-state tags.

"Well, look who it is!" said a large woman with a voice to match. She strolled up as if she owned the place, which of course she did.

"Hello, Holly," Randie said, a lilt of challenge in her tone. I wondered why, but not for long.

Holly wrapped Randie in a bone-crunching hug, and Randie crunched back. When their bodies finally separated, they left their hands locked in a sizzling grip that made them look like a couple of arm wrestlers sizing each other up for combat.

"What are you doing here, copper? My protection money is all paid up," Big Holly said loudly. Heads turned. The U.S. senator looked as though she was going to pass out.

"Haven't you heard? The rates are going up," Randie said.

Big Holly disengaged from their handshake and gestured at me. "What's this? A junior partner?"

"You guessed it," Randie said.

"So I have to start paying for her, too?"

"Not necessarily. Only if you want to save your kneecaps," Randie said.

Big Holly tried to say something back, but she couldn't keep herself from laughing. Randie laughed, too, and they got so silly about it they set most of the customers off, too, particularly the ones who clearly had seen this routine before. The senator looked vastly relieved.

"So this is Kotter," Big Holly said.

"Yeah, this is Kotter," I said. The handshake she gave me was gentle, not at all the bearlike squeeze she had given Randie, and I took the opportunity to get a good look at her. Big Holly's face was wide and open, her hair was red and pulled back, and her eyes were trusting, even though there was something in them that said her trust had been misplaced more than once. She seemed like someone who could handle the disappointment. I liked her, although of course I liked any friend of Randie's.

Big Holly put us at a favored table she had saved for the occasion — in a corner by one of the candle-lit windows. Randie and Jaws drank beer, and Julie had

Evian. I got the eye from Randie and drank Coke, even though I had learned to drink beer with the softball team last summer and Jaws and I had been sharing a bottle or two during our steamy sessions in her Mustang. Jaws took a long swallow, then leaned over and kissed me, and I loved the forbidden taste of it on her fervent lips. I had never kissed anyone in public before — Randie walking in on Shamrock and me didn't count — and I felt the stirrings deep inside. Jaws and I danced close and slow, but then Randie took Jaws aside and spoke earnestly to her, and it looked as though their talk would go on for a long time, so I danced affectionately with Julie. I did not know what Randie and Jaws discussed, and I never asked. It didn't matter, because I was sure nothing would go wrong.

Later we went back into the kitchen to meet Little Holly, and then Randie and Julie danced together, as electric as new lovers. In the course of the evening, it became natural to call Randie by her name, and another threshold was crossed.

The Hollies became very important in my life. Jaws and I went there a lot to dance and make the most of its dark and secret corners. Big Holly, who was the generous one, invited us to go into an unused room now and then, without charging us for it, and Little Holly, who had the business sense, didn't make a fuss.

That was the way things went into the spring, when I finally had the showdown with Wendell and Lynn about not going to college and fled the house. It was so irrevocably grave that Randie didn't even try to talk me into going back. Instead, she got the Hollies to take me in, giving me work in exchange for room and board and tips. Randie lent me money to buy a car and arranged for me to enroll in the criminal justice curriculum at the community college, starting in the summer session after I finished high school. I was on my way to being a cop.

Jaws graduated from Hillsboro College and went off to try out for the Olympic softball team. I was too busy to be lonely, and anyway, there were a lot of pretty women who made their way to the Hollies.

The next summer, when I was at Randie's and Julie's house, we watched the Olympics on television and saw that Jaws had, indeed, made the team. So had Shamrock. In fact, they were the winning battery — Shamrock pitching, Jaws catching — in the gold-medal game, won by the USA in a taut thriller, 1–0.

Afterwards, Randie chuckled. "You know what, Kotter?" she said. "I bet there isn't anyone on this earth who got laid by the Olympic team more than you."

CHAPTER SIX

Julie was pouring coffee. "I'll say this for you, Kotter, you sure have a knack for romancing world-class athletes. First Shamrock, then Jaws and now Alie de Ville."

"Who said anything about romancing Alie de Ville?" I protested.

Randie chuckled. "Come on, Kotter. Who do you think you're trying to kid?"

"How do you figure it, Randie?" Julie said. "What is it about Kotter that has them dying to get her in the sack?"

"Well, it sure isn't her good looks and personality," Randie needled. She gave me a once-over so searching it could have taken X-rays. "It's got to be that damn cocksure attitude. Those athletes have such an ego, they feel challenged, and they want to get her in bed and make her submit. You do submit, don't you, Kotter?"

"For Christ's sake, Randie!" I yelped.

The telephone rang. Randie glanced at the Caller ID. "Oh hell, it's the desk sergeant. This can't be good news." She picked up the receiver. "Hello? . . . Yes, Mac, what's up? . . . All right. Who's on it? . . . Tell Rashad to put Potter on it, too. I know he's supposed to have another day off, but the chief is going to have to show the mayor we're doing everything we can . . . Don't worry about that. I'll handle it. Tell them I'm on my way."

Randie hung up the phone. All the easiness of the evening had left her. She was a police captain again. "There was trouble at the tennis banquet tonight. A couple of goons jumped Papa de Ville in the parking lot while he was leaving. They got away. Now he's demanding more security for Alie, but she wants no part of it. Kotter, do you have a change of clothes with you?"

"Sure," I said. In this line of work, you always had to be prepared.

"Then come on. I need you. We've got to get to the College Inn."

I stood up — slowly — because it was all the time I would have for the transition back to duty. I wasn't Randie's friend Kotter anymore. I was just another officer to be deployed. I gave her the smirk, the one that said this cop could take anything the brass dished out. "Whatever you say, Captain."

She gripped my shoulder hard. "You sober?"

"Yeah." You had to hand it to Randie. She never missed anything.

"Then let's go. Follow me over to the station, and we'll pick up a car."

"I'll leave the light on," Julie said. She had grown too used to these abrupt departures to mind them very much.

At the station Randie slid into the passenger's seat of the cruiser, and I got behind the wheel. Off duty, she always drove, taking care of me, but when we were working, those captain's bars made it clear who would be doing what.

"The detectives don't have much to go on," Randie said. "No one got a good look at those guys who jumped Papa de Ville."

"Not even Papa?"

Randie was grim. "He's saying he didn't, but I wonder about that. Let's not forget, when Papa was growing up here, he was part of a pretty rough crowd. I'll bet he was attacked by a couple of locals with an old score to settle, but he doesn't want to admit it."

"Why wouldn't he?"

"Who knows? Pride? Fear? A feeling he had it coming? It could be anything."

"The chief will go nuts over this."

"You bet he will. He's going to want to keep it out of the press, too." Randie shook her head. She was part of the new breed of cop, the kind that thought exposure helped to catch crooks and keep the public trust. Chief Billy Wade was old school, secretive and damn near paranoid about anything getting out, maybe over-the-line paranoid if I thought about it too much.

"What are you going to do?"

Randie chuckled in spite of herself. "Probably call Penn."

Jonnie Penn was a reporter at the Hillsboro *Courier*. He joined the newspaper as a young police beat reporter almost to the day Randie was sworn in as a rookie cop. Outwardly he was a Clark Kent type — a mild-mannered reporter, painfully conscientious — but inside he was the man of steel, equipped with the laser instincts it took to get a story.

Randie met Penn in a chill, driving rainstorm at a particularly gory murder scene in the best part of town on a late October night. A teen-age kid had gotten himself drugged up and killed his father, who just happened to be the mayor's best friend and campaign treasurer. Since it was only a couple weeks until the election and the mayor was up for another term, the police brass were being particularly uncommunicative.

The reporters who flocked to the scene were largely satisfied by the promise of a press conference the next day in a dry and warm location, departing gratefully, but not Jonnie Penn. He stood in that miserable rain and waited for developments.

Randie was one of the officers assigned to secure the area. She saw him shivering just beyond the yellow police tape and approached him, not knowing who he was.

"It's a pretty awful night to be out," Randie said conversationally. "Isn't there someplace you'd rather be?"

"It's okayK. I'm a police reporter with the *Courier*. Jonnie Penn."

"Oh sure," Randie said sarcastically, skeptical of the name, "and I'm Janie Badge."

"No, really, it's my name," Penn said earnestly. He pulled out his wallet and displayed his press pass, identifying him as Jonathan Jefferson Penn.

Randie examined it, then smiled. "My mistake then. I'm Randie Wilkes. What are you still here for? There's going to be a press conference tomorrow."

Penn shrugged. "You never know what'll happen if you hang around."

Randie left him, the only figure at the crime scene who wasn't a cop. She parked herself gratefully inside a police car with the motor on and the heater running. Penn stood wretchedly in the downpour.

Not too much more time passed before Mayor Ernest G. Scrum arrived, shocked at his friend's death and panicked by his need for his campaign records and contributors' list. Penn was on him instantly, squeezing out a few pained quotes. The wait in the rain had been worth it. He had a hell of a story.

He also had Randie's immediate respect. It continued to grow through the years, finally leading to a special trust between them after the time she went undercover as a prostitute to nab the serial killer. Penn, being thorough as usual, was prowling around the seedy strip of highway the killer was believed to frequent. As he drove around in an unremarkable white Ford, he spotted her and stopped.

"Change professions?" he asked.

"You know what I'm doing."

"I sure do."

"Penn, if you write this, it will ruin everything. We're close to catching this guy. Real close. If you'll hold off, I promise I'll tip you when we make the arrest. You'll have it first."

Penn sighed. "My editor hates when we make deals. But throw in an interview about your part in it, and I'll do it."

Randie gestured with cherry-colored fingernails at her cheap clothes and gaudy jewelry. "An interview? No problem. I thought you were going to ask for a blow job."

Penn turned very, very red. He fumbled for his business card and slipped it to Randie. "The newsroom phone number is on there, and so is my home phone. I don't care when the arrest goes down, call me."

A week later, just after nightfall during a sweltering August heat wave, Randie made contact with the killer. He turned vicious more quickly than her backup expected, and she very nearly became the sixth victim before help arrived. Randie wound up in the hospital emergency room, but before she let the doctors treat her, she demanded a telephone. Her first call was to Julie, to let her know she was all right, and her second was to Penn. He hustled down to the police station, the only reporter there, and he knew too much for the public information officer to put him off. Penn broke the story in the morning paper and followed it up the next day with a searing account of Randie's role. She did the interview through stitches in her jaw, every syllable an aching challenge, but she did it. Penn had kept his word, and she would, too.

Randie got her arrest, and Penn got his blockbuster. They had counted on each other, and it made their reputations with their peers.

These days, however, Penn was long removed from the daily drudgery of the police beat. He covered more sweeping criminal justice stories and also did a lot of the *Courier*'s investigative reporting. Still, Randie could call him when she needed him, and Penn could do the same with her.

They kept their arrangement a secret — Randie because most other cops thought it was traitorous to consort with reporters, and Penn because that was what good reporters did for their sources. The only other cop besides me who knew about Penn was Sam Van Doren, the sergeant who was in charge of the security detail when I retrieved Alie de Ville from the airport. Like me, Sam was a special case. It was generally known that someday Randie would make chief, and when she did, Sam would be her second-in-command. There was no telling what I would do when Randie took over the department. I'd never been mistaken for leadership material.

Randie checked the time. "I'll call Penn when I can. He'll miss the early editions, but he ought to be able to get something in for the final." She chuckled. "He'll probably be asleep by the time I call. He never knows whether to love me or hate me when I do that. Anyway, he'll get his story, and the chief won't be able to hush it up."

I pulled into the College Inn, parked and followed

Randie into the lobby. It was furnished in the sort of stuffy, pretentious way favored by the academic set — perfect for impressing parents and aging alumni. My father, the vice president of finance, always entertained the biggest donors here. At least he used to. I hadn't had much contact with Wendell or Lynn since I left home.

The tennis crowd had been rough on the old lobby. It was a shambles of discarded hors d'oeuvres and half-drunk cocktails, tables with stained white linens and leftover name tags. It had the air of a grand dame who couldn't get her lipstick right anymore.

Then we heard the voice. It was coming from an alcove at the far end of the lobby, and it wasn't happy. It rankled in my head like a dentist's drill, but it also set my heart quivering and — well, never mind. It was Alie's voice, but my job was to concentrate on security.

"Is that her?" Randie asked incredulously.

"Yeah."

"She sounds like an alley cat."

"She's a tennis pro, not a TV anchor."

Randie grinned wickedly. "Well, I guess you can always turn up the music when the time comes, Kotter."

We entered the alcove. All was not well. Papa de Ville, his head and left hand in bandages, was looking at his daughter in exasperation. His tie was loosened, and there was blood on his white shirt, monogrammed on the cuff. Lieutenant Jim Ray Jones, the sort of musclehead cop that Alie hated, stood by forlornly with a couple of other officers from the ranks.

Alie glanced our way. When she saw me, she relaxed very slightly, like a race horse spotting its pony, but she tightened right up again. Despite her mood, she looked terrific. She was wearing a scoop-necked silk blouse, its dark color emphasizing her eyes and complementing her blond hair. The outline of her breasts showed teasingly through the soft fabric, which was tucked into very tight white dress slacks. Very tight. The blouse left matters to the imagination, but the slacks did not.

Randie double-clutched at the sight of her, I was happy to see, although it lasted too briefly for anyone else to notice. It wasn't every day you could throw Randie Wilkes off her stride.

The entry of a couple more cops had no impact at all on the de Villes. Alie was put out and letting everyone know it. "You said we were going to a hick town where nothing ever happened, and I could have some privacy for a change — no coach, no trainer, no bodyguard, nothing. I'm not putting up with a squad of cops wherever I go, and I'm certainly not letting one into my hotel suite, do you hear me?"

"Alessandra, you have to be sensible," Papa de Ville pleaded.

"You were the one who was attacked, not me. Anyway, you said you were just in the wrong place at the wrong time. Unless those guys were after you —"

"No, no," Papa stammered. Anyone with half a brain could tell he was lying.

"Then I don't want any security. If you make me, I'll just pull out of this dinky little tournament. I didn't want to play in it, anyway."

That got our attention. If Alie left, all the

glamour would go with her. The mayor would take it out on us, for sure. It was time for Randie to take charge.

"Mr. de Ville, I'm Captain Wilkes. Let's see what we can work out here."

Sure enough, Randie got it settled. Alie agreed I could provide her protection, as long as I didn't infringe on her privacy. Randie arranged for me to be lodged directly across the hall and got me a beeper for a quick summons.

That is how I came to be lying in a hotel room in my own town, naked and alone in a queen-sized bed. I stared at the blank expanse of white ceiling, distant and sterile, and pondered the cruel irony of life.

If anyone had told me I'd be spending the night in a hotel with the sexiest woman I'd ever met, I'd have said it was a dream come true.

Be careful what you wish for. Sometimes you need to be specific.

CHAPTER SEVEN

The telephone at my ear woke me early in the morning, leaving me startled and disoriented by the unfamiliar shapes in the hotel room. Daylight was just seeping around the curtains, and I wondered who the hell was calling so early.

I should have guessed. It was Alie, sounding damned pleased with herself. I wondered if I had grounds to arrest her for disturbing the peace.

"Get over here, Kotter! I've got practice at seven," she said. She was so chipper, she could have been a Mary Kay cosmetics lady at the door.

"Okay. On my way," I mumbled.

I glanced at the clock — it was quarter of six — then slipped into jeans and a T-shirt and padded barefoot across the hall. Alie answered my knock. The rising sun was framed in her window, making my eyes watery. It took me a moment to bring Alie into focus. As usual, I liked what I saw.

Alie was casual. She was wearing baggy sweatpants and an oversized T-shirt, but even those saggy clothes couldn't disguise the body underneath. Alie was one of those people who could look stylish in a pillow case with her hair dyed purple. I swear I was trying not to pay so much attention, but I just couldn't help myself. This babe was built.

"Come on in," she said. "Room service is bringing enough breakfast for two."

"A pleasant surprise."

"Oh, it has nothing to do with you. I just like a lot of variety to choose from. But you might as well have some."

I hated her. I was sure of it.

Alie busied herself by packing her tennis bag for her practice session. She didn't speak to me, and I didn't care.

The room service cart was delivered within minutes. I had never seen it arrive so quickly in any hotel, anywhere. I guess that's what it meant to be Alie de Ville.

I poured myself some coffee. She poured herself some fresh orange juice from a pitcher that in this place probably would have cost me about a day's pay.

The breakfast spread was quite lavish. Alie had ordered pancakes, oatmeal, scrambled eggs, assorted breads and a mess of fruit. I sloshed down the coffee and chewed on some toast, dry. I was a spartan at heart. Food had never held any particular attraction for me. The only time I got mildly interested was when Julie cooked, and that was because of Julie, not the food.

Alie grazed away, a little of this and a little of that, instant gratification, no attention span. I figured it was remarkable she remembered my name.

The hotel provided a copy of the Hillsboro *Courier* with breakfast. Alie let it lie folded until it got in her way as she reached for some jam. Then she picked it up and tossed it in the trash can.

"Hey, aren't you going to read that?" I asked.

"Why should I read it? If something's already in the paper, there's nothing I can do about it."

I was dumbfounded. I had never heard such logic. I had become quite the reader myself. Randie had done that to me in my youth. I read newspapers, magazines, novels and zillions of crime stories, fiction and nonfiction. Randie said I had become self-educated, which was a good thing, because I was otherwise unteachable.

I had taken exception when she said that. "You taught me."

"I trained you. Like a puppy at obedience school. And believe me, you weren't the top of the class."

I wondered, as I recalled that conversation, whether Randie would have gotten even that far with Alie. She really was terminally blonde.

Anyway, I wanted the newspaper. I was curious to see whether Penn had written anything about the assault on Papa de Ville. "Do you mind if I look at it?"

Alie waved her permission. Sure enough, Penn led

the paper. I bet there were a lot of important people mad at him for digging out the bad news — the mayor, the chief, the tournament officials, the Chamber of Commerce types and even the sports-writers, who got outhustled for the real story.

I scanned the police log — nothing I didn't already know about — checked the baseball scores and put the paper down.

Alie drained her coffee cup. "I need you to drive me out to that country club. What was it called? Buena Vista?"

"Yeah, Buena Vista. What do you have to go there for?"

"That's where I'm practicing. Daddy set me up for a session with the pro there. His name's Greg or Craig or something. Daddy thinks it's good for my image to be seen with a guy." She laughed.

"It's Gregg. Gregg with two *g*'s, as he's always telling everybody." I knew Gregg Clapham. He had tawny, flowing hair, a regular Bjorn Borg, and he changed his shirt on the court about a million times a day, so he could show off his pecs and abs. When he was in college, he was the top-ranked player in the state. He had the skills to make it on the pro tour, but he didn't have the cutthroat instincts. He settled for being a teaching pro, making decent but not spectacular money at the Buena Vista Country Club. He did have the tennis pro looks, though. Papa de Ville knew what he was doing when he set Alie up with Gregg.

I was surprised Alie was practicing at Buena Vista. The tournament was at Hillsboro College, which had a stadium tennis court with bleachers.

"You're not practicing at the college? I thought you had to get used to the surface you're playing on."

Alie gave me a look. "Have you seen the draw for this tournament? My first match is with a qualifier from the college. I could beat her on a court made of green cheese. This isn't exactly Wimbledon, you know."

"Sorry. When do you want to leave? I have to get cleaned up and check in with the desk sergeant."

Twenty minutes later we were headed for the country club, Alie in the back of the police car and me in the front, feeling like a chauffeur again. All I needed was a cap and a pair of driving gloves.

"What happened with your father last night?" I asked.

"You're the cop. You're the one who should know."

"All I know is I was pulled away from a very nice dinner and ordered back on duty. I didn't exactly have time to find out too much."

"He was mugged. That's all."

"When?"

"After the banquet. He went out to the parking lot to go back to the condo, and two guys came up to him before he got to his car. They wanted his wallet, and he fought with them, and they beat him up and then they ran away."

"Did they get his wallet?"

"No."

"How come they ran away? Did he yell for help?"

Alie sighed. "What is this, the third degree?"

"Okay, never mind. I was just curious." I sure was curious. Papa de Ville's story sounded fishy to me. If two guys want your wallet and they beat you up, they take it. And why didn't Papa holler? I had a feeling Randie was right — Papa knew who his attackers were and had a reason to conceal it.

I stopped at a red light. Alie got fidgety. "Can't you put on your lights and siren and get moving?"

"Not without cause. I'd have to arrest you first."

"What for?" She sounded playful.

"Oh, I don't know. How about 'interfering with the duties of a police officer'?"

"Don't you wish," Alie said. The next thing I knew, she leaned forward and softly stroked the back of my neck. It was a silken jolt I was utterly unprepared for. My body didn't know whether to stiffen or sag.

"Now can you drive faster?" Alie spoke so softly, the buzz saw was nearly out of her voice.

"No." I needed all the reserves I had for that one syllable. Alie was sending currents through my body that were draining me of will power, and I didn't exactly have much of a record for refusing attractive women.

Abruptly the hand and the golden touch were withdrawn, and I got the silent treatment the rest of the way to the country club. I was glad I had said no.

Buena Vista was quiet at this hour of the day, except for some diehard foursomes of golfers and the maintenance staff starting its shift. Julie wouldn't arrive for a couple of hours.

The tennis courts weren't officially open so early, but Gregg was there, waiting for Alie. He was shirtless, of course. I let Alie out of the police car, and she stalked by me like a Wicked Stepsister passing

96

Cinderella. Well, she better not ask to borrow my glass slippers.

I could have done the introductions for Alie and Gregg, but I didn't bother. Instead, I lounged by the police car as Alie did a pretty fair job of flirting with him. Then they got down to tennis, and I forgot all about how irritated I was.

No model, no gymnast, no dancer in her prime had more grace than Alie de Ville with a tennis racquet. She was poetry for the eye and ballet for the soul, her movements flowing and steady and sure. No matter how hard Gregg drilled balls at her, no matter how much he mixed up the pace, she was as unfaltering as a clock moving through time.

Alie was a serve-and-volleyer, a style that distinguished her from most of the baseliners on the women's tour. I became particularly enamored of her serve, the ball tossed high in the summer air, one arm pointing skyward while the other cocked the racquet, the breasts lifted, the knees bending under the strong thighs. The moment would hold and hold and hold, until the serve exploded and Alie rocketed back to life.

I experienced the wonder that Adam must have felt as he looked at Eve, a creature like him and yet somehow apart, always to be yearned after and never captured. Alie on a tennis court was something different from you and me.

The impatient, pouting prima donna was nowhere to be seen, replaced by this earthly angel. It was hard to believe the two could exist in the same body. I found myself smiling. I bet Alie didn't even know what a gift she had. Like everything else in her life, it was just another gratification, there for the asking.

Alie and Gregg worked hard out there, and when they were finished, they walked side by side into the clubhouse to get something to drink. I wasn't included, but I was supposed to be providing security, so I followed. I kept my distance, though.

Eventually Alie said good-bye and steered my way. The glow from the tennis court was still on her. "Could you take me back to the hotel, please?" she said, unexpectedly transformed into a clone of Miss Manners.

"Sure."

I got on the radio to let the desk sergeant know where we were heading. The Beer Belly Polka was on duty. He told me I'd be relieved at the hotel and to report to the station. Randie wanted to see me.

"Will you be back to take me to my match this evening?" Alie asked.

"I assume so. That was the original plan."

"I want to go out after I play. Gregg says the hottest place in town is Poe's."

That was true. The nightspot near the college campus had as its slogan, "We'll have you 'raven' evermore!" It was loud and rowdy and gave us more trouble than any other legal place in Hillsboro, mostly because of the rough male townies who got themselves drunk and then tried either to pick up the college women or pick fights with the college men. Recently Poe's had changed management and gotten even worse. The new owner was trying to draw more business with wet T-shirt contests and female mud wrestling acts. He wanted to have an amateur strippers night, but the mayor threatened to shut him down over that one, and he backed off.

The last thing I needed was to keep track of Alie

de Ville in a place like that. Fortunately I had a reason to keep her away. "Sorry. You can't get in there if you're under twenty-one."

"What bullshit! Come on, Kotter, don't be a prude."

"No way."

"You could go as my date."

I looked in the rear view mirror and gave her the smirk. "You never give up, do you?"

"I'll take that for a 'yes.' "

"It wasn't."

Alie smiled dreamily. She seemed very sure of herself.

Sam Van Doren met us at the College Inn. I didn't like how serious he seemed. "What's going on, Sam?"

"Trouble. Randie will tell you."

Sam was nothing if not loyal. I wouldn't get another word out of him if Randie hadn't authorized him to speak. It was one of the reasons she trusted him. She knew she could always count on him to do what he was supposed to do.

I felt my heart start pumping with the fear and exhilaration that danger always brings. If you couldn't get scared and enjoy it, you were in the wrong business.

"Okay, Sam. Alie's all yours, and believe me, you're welcome to her. I'm on my way."

CHAPTER EIGHT

The Beer Belly Polka leered at me as I walked past the desk. "Hey, Kotter, I hear that blonde bombshell is making you jump through all sorts of hoops. We should have sent a man out for that job."

"Yeah, Sarge, she's making me jump, dive, do backflips, whatever." I poked him in the famous belly. "But at least I can fit through those hoops, you know what I mean?"

"Kotter, I swear, one of these days I'm going to write you up!"

I left him, still quivering, and walked into

Randiee's office. "Did I hear you and Cranshaw mixing it up again?" she asked.

"Affirmative. I stuck a finger in his gut. I feel like I just molested the Pillsbury Doughboy."

Randie laughed before she could stop herself. "Cut it out, Kotter."

"Sorry. What's going on? Sam said there's trouble."

"There is." Randie picked up a sheet of paper. "When Potter went to Papa de Ville's condo this morning to ask him some more questions, there was a note taped to the door. Here's a photocopy. The original's already gone to the FBI."

"The FBI?" I repeated. This was serious. I took the paper from Randie. Letters from newspapers and magazines had been cut out childishly and pasted to form the words:

mONiCa SELes got OFf eAsY.

There was no mistaking what the message meant. Monica Seles was the tennis player who was stabbed in the back by a deranged fan during a match in Germany. Whoever had a grudge against Papa de Ville was threatening to carry it out on his daughter.

"What do you think?" Randie asked.

I glanced at the cutouts again. "I think someone's been reading too many Dick Tracy comics."

"Anything else?"

"Yeah. It looks like this note was put together right in town. Most of the letters are in the type the *Courier* uses."

"I noticed that, too."

"So now what?"

101

"Now it gets complicated. Papa de Ville wants more security for Alie, but he doesn't want her to know about the note. He says it would affect her tennis."

"And we're going along with that?"

"We have to. That's what the mayor told the chief. The mayor will do anything to save this tournament."

I winced. It was hard enough to protect someone without worrying about politics; with it, security was as risky as Russian roulette.

"What about telling Penn?"

"Not this time. There aren't enough people who know about it. A leak would be too easy to trace."

"Damn."

"It's going to put a lot of pressure on you. Stay with her, Kotter. I'll make sure you have backup, but you're the first line of defense."

"I take it the detectives haven't turned up anything."

"No. Papa de Ville is still stonewalling, insisting he didn't recognize his attackers. We're asking questions around town, but Papa's been gone a long time. It's hard finding people who knew him, let alone people who are out to get him."

"You want me to ask Alie about it?"

"Better not. Papa doesn't want her to know anything about this, and the mayor's on his side."

"We're really fucked, aren't we?"

Randie chuckled. "Not fucked, Kotter. Sold down the river on account of money and politics. You get fucked when someone wants to hurt you. You get sold when you don't matter enough to get fucked."

"Here I thought you were just a police captain, and it turns out you're a philosopher, too."

Randie smiled. "Well, the lecture's over. It's time to get back to your tennis star. And leave through the back of the station so you don't go by Cranshaw again. I don't have time to listen to him bitch about you."

I stopped at my place and got enough clothes for the next four days, which would take me beyond the end of the tournament until the players left town. I figured I would be at the College Inn for the duration.

I found Sam Van Doren in the hallway outside Alie's room. "How's it going?" I asked.

"No problems. She had lunch with a couple of the other players, and then they went out by the pool. She came back up here about an hour ago and hung the 'Do Not Disturb' sign on the door, and she's been quiet ever since."

"What did you do, Sam, slip her some Valium?"

"Just lucky, I guess. She's been giving you a hard time, hasn't she? I heard you had to be up at the crack of dawn this morning."

"If anybody's thinking about kidnapping her, they ought to talk to me first."

Sam smiled, but then he got serious. "Well, she's all yours. I have to get back to the station. I've got a long stretch ahead. I'm going to get out the old police reports, dating to the time her father lived here, and see if he shows up in anything. Wouldn't you know the guy left town before the records were computerized."

"That's not going to be easy."

"Tell me about it. See you later."

I unlocked my room across the hall from Alie's and left the door open. I put my stuff away and loafed around, waiting for the next summons. She surfaced in late afternoon and surprised me with a welcoming smile.

"Kotter! Can you take me over to the tournament? I want to hit some more before I play tonight."

I was really keyed up. This was the first time I had Alie out in public since the trouble began. I was furious with Papa de Ville, too. If he'd given us a description of those goons, we'd know if they showed up. This way they had the jump on us.

Alie was spotted as soon as we arrived. I had to hand it to her, she was good with the crowds. She kept moving, but she talked and signed autographs as she went. Since Hillsboro was pretty awestruck at having her here, no one got rude, and we didn't have any problems.

I was relieved to find the place blanketed with cops, most of them in uniform to be visible. I personally was in my blue suit and a new pair of sunglasses, doing my imitation of the Secret Service. All I lacked was one of those little buttons to talk into and a wire in my ear.

Alie went into the locker room, hooked up with a player I didn't recognize, and then the two of them headed for a practice court. Within minutes there was a crowd, pressed against the chain link fence to watch. I think Alie had more people watching her warm up than did the two low-ranking pros playing the afternoon match.

Alie seemed restless, though. She wandered amid the practice courts, the dining hall and the locker room until it was time for her to go on.

Of course, she was the featured match of the night. Dusk was closing in as she entered the stadium court, the contrast between the growing darkness and the bright lights making it hard for me to scan the capacity crowd. Damn Papa de Ville, anyway.

People stood and cheered, but Alie was all business. She didn't even glance at her father, sitting in a courtside box with the mayor, the diamond stick pin in his tie catching the light. Papa looked expansive. This tournament was obviously everything he wanted it to be — recognition, vindication, a gloating glory. It only remained to be seen how dear a price he would pay for it.

The next box over from Papa and the mayor belonged to the college president. I noticed my parents sitting there, along with a couple of trustees and some rich old alumni. We didn't so much as nod.

Alie was playing Tammy Truman, the top Hillsboro College player who got into the tournament as a courtesy to the school. Poor Tammy got mugged out there. After she lost the first set 6–1, she took a white bandanna out of her tennis bag and waved it in surrender. The crowd loved it, and I saw a bunch of white handkerchiefs waving back in sympathy. Alie played along, aiming her racquet like a rifle at Tammy. The cameras flashed, and that was the picture on the front page of the *Courier* in the morning. No wonder Alie was so popular. She had talent and style — if you didn't know her.

Then Alie finished what she started, mowing down Tammy 6–0 in the second set to win the match. She was a killer, that was for sure.

I lounged by the door to the locker room as I waited for Alie to change. She didn't take long, blowing into view like a model off a runway, dressed in jeans, a white shirt and a bright, multi-colored vest. The vest, left unbuttoned, also left no doubt she wasn't wearing a bra.

Everything about her said she was on the prowl. I used to see that look all the time when I was with Jaws, the one that athletes got after they won and were ready to collect their trophies. It had been the cause for some pretty torrid nights in the sack. There was one time after Jaws won a softball game in the last at-bat with a grand slam . . . wow.

Alie saw the glow of memory in my eyes and took it for admiration. She smiled smugly as I escorted her to the police car. "Ready for Poe's?" she asked.

I came back to reality in a hurry. I slammed the door so she couldn't escape from the backseat and got in to drive. "I told you. I can't take you there."

"Then just drop me off. You can say you don't know where I am."

"Are you nuts? I'm not allowed to let you out of my sight."

"Look, just take the poker out of your ass and let's go. Who's going to know?"

"Oh sure, like you're not the most famous person in Hillsboro and no one will notice you. Listen, I am not going to lose my badge for you."

Alie slitted her eyes. The screech in her voice was as bad as I'd heard it. "If you don't take me there, I'll see that you do lose your badge."

I'm sure Alie expected me either to wilt or get mad. What she didn't know was that I was never more relaxed than when I was threatened. After a lifetime of being in trouble, it was my natural habitat.

I startled her by simply laughing. I put the car in gear and headed out.

"Where are you taking me? Where are you taking me?" she demanded.

I ignored her and drove to the College Inn. Alie was a thundercloud of silence. I parked and let her out. She fled upstairs and slammed the door to her room. I opened the door to mine and prepared to wait until the bars shut down at one a.m.

Time passed, and then I heard the elevator stop. It discharged Tammy Truman, the college player Alie had slaughtered earlier in the evening. Alie must have called her. Tammy went to Alie's door and knocked. She was carrying a package that only could have contained a six-pack of beer.

Well, Tammy was of age, and I was damned if I was going to play dorm mother to see who drank it.

Alie's door opened only wide enough to admit Tammy. I stayed on alert to see whether they tried to slip out on me, but they didn't. They had a room service cart delivered with food and a bottle of wine, but that was it for the night.

After one a.m., I called the officer on duty in the lobby and said I was turning in. I was mildly curious about whether Tammy was going to stay, but I hadn't had much sleep the night before and I was tired.

The hell with it, I thought, and the hell with Alie, too.

CHAPTER NINE

For the second morning in a row, the telephone woke me before the sun did.

"What?" I snarled, expecting the call to be from Alie, but it was Randie. Big mistake.

"Be in my office in fifteen minutes," she said in a tone of cold command.

"Fifteen minutes!"

"One of the officers in the lobby will relieve you. Don't be late."

Once again I was stumbling and rushing, half

asleep, as I sped through the shower and got ready. I had no idea what I had done to get the recruit-class treatment, but I was irritated and more than willing to play the part. I pulled on jeans and a faded Police Academy T-shirt, skipped the socks and didn't bother to tuck the shirt in.

I don't think I made it in fifteen minutes, but I was probably standing in front of Randie's desk in seventeen. Whatever, it was close enough. I saluted and said nonchalantly, "You sent for me, Captain?"

"Sit down, Kotter."

Randie didn't look happy. She was in full uniform, and I had the sense that as early as she got me up, she had been up a lot earlier. I knew she wouldn't be in the mood for any lip from me, but I wasn't real optimistic that I would be able to control it. I draped myself insolently in a chair.

"I have just come from a rather unpleasant session with the mayor and the chief, and you were the cause of it. It seems Alie complained to her father that you were rude and arrogant last night, and her father called the mayor. He called the chief, and the chief called me, and the three of us had a little get-together. Now I'd like to give you the benefit of the doubt, except I heard the way you sounded on the phone this morning."

I winced. "I shouldn't have answered like that. I'm sorry. But I wasn't rude to Alie last night. She wanted to go to Poe's, and I wouldn't let her. Or did the law change when I wasn't paying attention, Captain?"

"From now on, whatever Alie wants, you do."

"You cannot be serious."

"I offered to remove you from this assignment, but it seems Alie made it quite clear she wants you to continue."

"She said she'd get me."

"Then don't give her any more chances to do it."

"God damn it, I don't mind being in trouble when I've done something wrong, but it sure as hell shouldn't happen when I've done something right!"

"Enough, Kotter. You're dismissed."

I stood and snapped my best recruit-class salute. It was a gesture of obedience turned into flagrant insubordination, and Randie gave me a stare as cold as Judgment Day. I glared back until I finally wised up and dropped my gaze. I was scared I really had gone too far this time. When would I ever learn to control that temper?

"You're your own worst enemy," Randie said. If there was no forgiveness in her voice, there was at least awareness, and I was grateful for that much.

"I know it, Captain."

I stopped in the break room to collect myself and pick up a cup of coffee. It didn't help that I hadn't had any yet this morning. Although Randie had dressed me down, I knew she would have done everything she could to cover for me with the chief and the mayor. If I screwed up, I would hurt her as much as myself, and I wasn't going to do that to her.

God, I could just kill Alie de Ville.

I returned to the College Inn and the tyranny that awaited me there. I went upstairs and saw Corporal Steve Ortega in the hallway. I liked Steve. He was another of Randie's reclamation projects, like me. One of his cousins had played softball with me, and she introduced Steve to Randie. At the time Steve's parents were divorcing, his grades were going to hell, and he was getting in so much trouble at school he was flirting with expulsion. Randie was the first to see the gentleness inside and Steve's need for order. She invited him to join her criminal justice program for high school students, then in its early days. That's where I met him, and we had been friends ever since.

Steve was a bruiser of a man, the strongest weightlifter in the police department. His uniforms had to be custom made, and still his shoulders rippled beneath the thin blue fabric. The first time I ever called for backup, when some passengers got unruly during a drunken-driving stop, Steve was the first one on the scene. That's not something you ever forget.

"Hey, Ortega. Any sightings of Herself yet?"

"Nope. Room service delivered about twenty minutes ago. I saw more food on that cart than I could even eat."

I wondered whether Tammy still was inside, but I didn't mention it. "That's the way she likes breakfast. She grazes."

"She's really giving you a hard time, isn't she? It's all anybody's talking about at the station."

"She really is. She's got me in trouble with the chief and even the mayor, if you can believe it."

"As if you needed help getting in trouble," Steve teased. "What happened?"

Before I could answer, my beeper sounded. Alie was calling. "Later," I told him.

Steve glanced at his watch and yawned. "Well, I'm off. Been working all night. It's Miller time."

"Breakfast of champions."

Steve grinned and headed for the elevator. I knocked on Alie's door. "It's open," I heard her say, and I went in, wondering what I would find there — the lady or the tiger?

The suite had suffered since I was last inside. It was littered with the debris from the night before — discarded clothes, empty beer cans, trays of food and the dead soldier of a wine bottle. It had that distinct, stale after-party pungency to it.

Tammy was not in evidence, but Alie sure as hell was. She was dressed in a white terry cloth robe and nothing else that I could see. Her long legs were exposed by the slash in the robe, and the neckline veered into dangerous territory. Even though I was furious with her, I could feel those prickly sensations that come on when you are near a woman who is hot, hot, hot. Where Alie was concerned, I couldn't even count on my own body.

"Well?" she asked.

"You win," I said tersely. "Wherever you want to go, you go. Whatever you want to do, you do. I am at your service."

"I told you."

"Are you going to rub this in?"

"As a matter of fact, I am. I think you should apologize."

Most people hate to say they're sorry. Not me. I can't think of a cheaper way to get out of a jam. I apologize when I'm right, I apologize when I'm wrong, I apologize any way I can to strong women who get turned on by it. I've apologized a million times and never meant it. Alie de Ville could have her apology without a qualm from me.

"I am deeply and truly sorry," I said and did not smirk.

That pleased her. She gave me a superior smile, and then she stretched. Her body moved, but the robe didn't, and the tops of her breasts came rising like twin moons above the rough texture of the terry cloth, soft half-circles out of a coarse, slashing V. I watched and did not bother to hide that I was watching, as she prolonged the pose, making damn sure she was tantalizing me.

I should have been striding across the room, peeling back the robe, whispering crude desires to her and doing unspeakable things to her body. But I was not the one who could say what would happen here. I felt like a caged wolf.

The stretch ended. The moons sank below the horizon, and I was jarred back to all that is gritty and barren by the ungodly pitch in her voice. "I have to be out at Buena Vista again this morning. I'm playing golf with my father and my agent and some corporate bigwig who's thinking about sponsoring me." She made a face. "I told my father I didn't want to do any business this week, but he said this guy was flying in special. Anyway, what else is there to do in this diddly little town?"

"Well, the college library has a display of medieval manuscripts, but I don't think that's what you had in mind."

Alie giggled. "God, you have a smart mouth."

The better to — I thought it, but I didn't say it.

In forty minutes we were on our way to Buena Vista, Alie in the back seat just as chipper as she could be. Either she got laid last night, or else this babe really got off on power trips like the one she pulled on me.

Of course, she looked exquisite in her little plaid golf shorts and white shirt with matching plaid collar. I was doing my Secret Service imitation again — tan suit and sunglasses.

Buena Vista was an armed camp of cops, and I wasn't needed. I got permission from the sergeant in charge to knock off as long as Alie was on the golf course. I headed for Julie's office.

She was in the back with a client. I helped myself to some coffee — hazelnut this morning — and before I had drained the cup, the client emerged. She was one of those blue-haired ladies who kept Julie comfortably in business. This one swept by me with a look that said I may have youth, but she had money, and one day my youth would be gone but her money wouldn't. It wasn't the first time I had seen that look from one of Julie's clients.

Julie followed a moment or two later. "Kotter! What are you doing here? Hey, what's wrong? You're not looking so good."

"I was insubordinate."

"Oh! You poor baby." If anybody else had said that — including Randie — I would have cut it off and said something obscene. But not Julie. She was a healer, and her sympathy was neither pitying or patronizing. It was what I needed.

I told her of the morning's events, and I was as hard on myself as Randie would have been. As I spoke, Julie helped me out of my suit jacket and

114

then massaged my neck and shoulders and upper back, until the tension and my words drained and drained and drained away all at the same time.

"Don't worry, Kotter. I'll take care of this with Randie for you."

"I don't know how you do it."

Julie smiled mischievously. "Let's just say I have a few more tricks at my disposal than you do."

I drank coffee with Julie until her next client arrived, and then I wandered into the clubhouse lobby and shot the bull with some of the other cops. About the time I figured Alie should be finishing up her round of golf, the sergeant came looking for me.

"Someone else will take Alie de Ville back to the hotel," he told me. "You're to report to Captain Wilkes at the station."

I wondered why. What I didn't know was that all hell had broken loose. At least this time it had nothing to do with me.

CHAPTER TEN

When I walked into Randie's office, she was waiting at the door for me. She put her hand on the back of my neck, and my breath caught, but there was no anger in her touch. It meant I was already out of the doghouse and on probation. I relaxed. Julie would take care of the rest.

Randie fingered the collar and lapel of my jacket. "How many suits did you buy for this assignment?"

"Two," I lied. Actually I had bought three — the blue one, this tan one and a dark green one — but the green was only for emergencies in case one of the

116

others got stained or torn. The odds were good Randie would only see me in the blue and the tan. "I can always use them when I make detective."

"By the time you make detective," Randie said drily, "these suits are going to be out of style."

"Very funny, Captain," I said, giving her the cop's smirk.

"Detective!" Randie was chuckling now. "When you finish this assignment, you'll be lucky if I let you write parking tickets on Main Street. School crossing duty is going to look like a perk to you."

It was time for me to remember my right to remain silent. There was no sense giving Randie any more ammunition. I wondered what had happened since the morning to turn her mood around. I didn't have to wait long to find out.

Randie shut the door — something she rarely did — and said, "There's going to be a briefing for the entire security detail later on, but I want you to know what led up to it. Obviously anything I tell you stays here."

"Sure. What's going on?"

"Penn. Jonnie Penn. He's screwed everything up. The chief and the mayor are furious, and so is Papa de Ville." Randie seemed quite pleased about it, too.

"Let's see," I said. "Does this mean that along with repealing the drinking age for Alie, the chief and the mayor are going to want to repeal the freedom of the press, too?"

"God damn it, Kotter, you are incorrigible!" Randie said, and then she laughed. As a matter of fact, in all the years I had known her, I don't think I ever saw her laugh so hard or so long. I had her wiping away tears.

"All right," she finally said. "Let me tell you what happened. The only one I feel sorry for in all this is Sam Van Doren. Poor Sam. He stayed up all night, going through those old police records without finding a thing, and then Penn figured it out from old newspaper stories. I swear, if Penn ever wants to quit the *Courier,* I'd hire him in a minute.

"Our hunch was right. Papa de Ville hung around with some pretty shady characters when he was growing up in Hillsboro. Penn found an old file on him in the newspaper library. Papa was involved in one of the worst scandals ever to hit this town, back when he was in high school. Probably not very many people remember he was a part of it, but I bet the chief does — he was just starting out on the force at the time. I bet the mayor does, too.

"Anyway, a bunch of young toughs put a gambling ring together and bet on high school football games. Eventually they tried to talk some of the Hillsboro players into throwing a game, and one of the players went to the coach. To make a long story short, everyone in the gambling ring was kicked out of school for the rest of the year.

"The newspaper story said Papa was a junior at the time, but it doesn't look like he ever went back. Penn called the high school, and there's no record he graduated.

"There's nothing else on Papa in the *Courier* library, but there were stories about some of the others in the gambling ring who went on to rougher stuff — burglaries, bad checks, small-scale drug dealing, assaults during bar fights, the usual.

"Penn called me this morning to tell me what he

had found, and we talked off the record. He wanted to know if we had anything else on Papa or these other guys, but I told him he'd done a better job than we had. He asked if I thought Papa's old pals could be the ones who jumped him, and I said that's sure as hell where I'd start.

"Later Penn called the chief to get an official comment and to tell him he was writing a story about Papa's past in Hillsboro. The chief freaked, and that's when the fun started."

"Great story," I said. "Father of tennis star gets his start in sports by betting on them."

"Exactly. Penn's out there trying to get comments from the mayor, Papa de Ville and his old cronies. Meanwhile, the mayor's been on the phone with the publisher, trying to get the story killed, and Papa's threatening to sue the paper if they print it and cancel the tennis tournament."

"What do you think will happen?"

"Oh, you know the newspapers. They'll run the story."

"Let me guess. The chief says the story will screw up our investigation, and you say the more people who know about it, the better chance we have of protecting Papa and Alie and cracking this crime."

"You're learning, Kotter."

"So now what?"

"Now at least we have the names of Papa's old pals. Recognize anyone?"

Randie handed me a list of a dozen names, and I scanned it. "I arrested a guy named William Gibbons a couple months ago for credit card fraud, but he was young. Maybe a son or a nephew or something."

"Maybe. It's a pretty common name, though. We have mug shots on some of these characters, but nothing recent. Still, it's a start.

"The briefing is in an hour. Sam's going to conduct it, although I'll come by. Be there." Randie put a hand on my shoulder, captain to cop. "Don't you forget about our talk this morning. You have your orders. This changes nothing."

"Yes, ma'am."

I got back to the College Inn in time to drive Alie to the tournament. Like the day before, she wanted to get there early. I noticed she was edgy again, like a thoroughbred approaching the starting gate.

"Is everything okay?" I asked, wondering whether Papa had told her about Penn's discoveries.

"Oh, I always get nervous before a match. It doesn't matter if I'm playing a qualifier or Steffi. I used to throw up, even. Now I just always think I'm going to lose, and then I go out on the court and something comes over me and I get fierce and I win. It's like Wonder Woman or something."

I figured that was as profound as Alie de Ville got. I left her to her thoughts. I kept an eye on her until match time, and then I wandered courtside and took up a position just behind the low wall that separated the court from the crowd. I had memorized the few mug shots we had, and I felt much more comfortable as I checked out the scene. I noticed the other cops seemed more confident, too. There was no guarantee, of course, that Papa's muggers were local, and we might be entirely off the track. Still, we felt we had accomplished something.

Papa and the mayor showed up a little before Alie was scheduled to appear for the traditional, pre-match warmup. Shortly after they arrived, so did Penn. He had press credentials around his neck and a notebook in his hand as he approached the mayor's box. He said something, and the mayor, who had his fill long ago of Penn's embarrassing stories, turned in fury. Papa stood up and shook his fist, unleashing the street punk that loomed inside the multi-millionaire. Penn raised his hands in a gesture of apology and retreated. It sure looked like a couple of "no comments" to me. I had to admire Penn. He did a lot of the unpleasant things we did — and without a badge or backup.

The players emerged to a standing ovation. Alie was going against one of those fifteen-year-old sensations who should still be in high school, not trying to make it on the tour. Her opponent had a bunch of weapons, but she was too young to be consistent with them. She would follow up a spectacular shot with a total muff job — which certainly kept the match interesting. Alie had the patience to let her make her mistakes and walloped her in straight sets, 6–3, 6–3.

Now it was my turn to be nervous and maybe a little bitter. Alie came out of the locker room, signed some autographs and said to me, "Take me to Poe's."

I nodded, feeling sorely used. Alie might not take prisoners on a tennis court, but she sure as hell took hostages in real life.

Alie looked hot to trot. She was dressed in another one of those silky shirts, this one in green, which might as well have had a road map pointing, "This way to the nipples." She also wore khaki jeans, neatly pressed, just begging to be stripped off and rumpled. Walking into Poe's, she would be a knock-out even if she wasn't Alie de Ville. She wasn't making it easy on the cop assigned to security, I can tell you that.

Poe's was packed, its primal rock music pulsating into the parking lot every time the door was opened, which was frequently. I took a look at the customers and realized the tennis tournament managed to coin-cide with the summer practice for Hillsboro College's football team. Huge, swaggering college boys were everywhere, the kind the locals resented. Damn. Poe's was going to be its combustible worst.

I let Alie out of the car and followed her toward the door. She stopped and said, "I don't want you too close to me. I don't need any nanny."

"Okay."

She grabbed my lapel playfully. "Unless, of course, you want to have a drink with me, Kotter."

"No, ma'am, I'm on duty."

"Fuck you, Kotter." She shoved me aside and walked away. Her hips were rocking.

Inside people had to turn sideways and shoulder their way through the gyrating crowd. Alie spotted some other tennis pros at the bar and bulldozed toward them. They were encircled by a panting crew of football players.

It took a moment for the crowd to realize Alie was Alie. Heads turned, fingers pointed, and there was a general surge in her direction, although not many people got through. I took advantage of the disruption to wedge myself against the wall near the door. If I couldn't stay close to Alie, at least I could prevent her from leaving without me. I settled in grimly for a long and miserable evening.

In Alie's little group she quickly became the center of attention. She joked with the other tennis players, flirted with the football studs and even kissed the bartender. She drank way, way too much.

The night wore on. The music got louder and more frantic. A couple of the other tennis players left, but not Alie. By this time, she was drunk enough to be leaning against the bar for support. One of the football types, the biggest and blondest among them, helped her toward the rest rooms in the rear. At first when they didn't return right away, I wondered whether there was a line. Then I wondered whether Alie was sick. Then I broke out in a cold sweat as I wondered whether they had gone out the emergency exit. If the alarm went off, no one would have heard it in this din.

I shot out the door and sprinted toward the back. I saw them in a corner of the parking lot. The football player had Alie pinned against a pickup truck, his hands groping wherever they wanted, his mouth covering hers. She was struggling, but she couldn't get away.

I ran up to them. "Police! Let her go."

The football player turned partially toward me but still kept a hand on Alie's hip. The guy was easily six-foot-four, and he was drunk. He took one look at me and laughed. "Go fuck yourself, copper," he said.

He shouldn't have done that. I was carrying a blackjack. It was no longer regulation, and I wasn't supposed to have one. If I got caught with it, I'd be in trouble, but sometimes you do what you have to do.

A blackjack was a joy to use. You could conceal it in your hand and then smash it with all your might against an elbow, even one belonging to a guy who was six-foot-four, and watch as the excruciating pain left him crumpled and howling. Stick it as hard as you could into his gut, and you had really made your point.

As he doubled over, trying to clutch his stomach and his elbow at the same time, I snarled my identification at him. "Kotter, W.L., Hillsboro P.D., badge number two-four-six-oh-one. Go ahead and turn me in."

I knew he wouldn't. There was no way a guy like him would ever let it be known he had been whipped by a female cop like me.

Alie stumbled into my arms. I helped her across the parking lot to the police car. "Can I sit up front?" she sniffled. I let her in the passenger's side, then got behind the wheel. "Can we just sit here a minute, please?" she asked.

She cried quietly, not really making a big deal out of what had happened, just getting her emotions out. I felt my adrenaline level returning to normal.

"You were right," she said wanly. "I shouldn't have come to Poe's."

I forgave her for everything. I was nothing if not a pushover for a beautiful damsel I had just saved from distress. Isn't that the way it works in all the fairy tales?

"Listen," I said. "I know a place we can go that

will make you feel better. It's called the Hollies. It's for women."

"My father will kill me if I'm seen in a place like that."

"No one will know. It's very discreet. I've been going there for years."

"If you're really sure, then okay."

I drove out the dark, familiar road to the inconspicuous break in the low stone wall, up the twisted drive through the press of pine trees to the inn with the single candles shining in the windows, the inn that had become my home when there was no more home to be had with Wendell and Lynn. This is where I grew up, where I learned what it meant to be included in the company of women. If there was such a thing as ghosts, mine would return here when the time came, sharing eternity with the shades of Randie and Julie and the Hollies, the women who took me in.

Alie could have let herself out, but she waited for me to help her. "This is pretty," she said.

We went inside, and immediately I was swallowed by Big Holly's bearlike embrace. When she released me, she greeted Alie with the experience that came from welcoming scores of closeted celebrities. Then she wagged her finger at me. "Kotter! Why didn't you phone ahead? I'd have reserved a table for you. Fortunately, I have one set aside. I had a feeling this tennis tournament could produce a few extras."

"Sorry, Holly, but this was a spur-of-the-moment thing."

Holly hugged me and whispered in my ear, "With your talents, Kotter, I'm not surprised."

I shrugged, content to let her think whatever she wanted to. Big Holly was happily paired with Little Holly, but she had never missed a chance to lay a hand on me. Just being friendly, of course.

She showed us to a table nearer the front than she usually put me, then excused herself to greet some other new arrivals. I glanced around. It was mostly a hometown crowd. I noticed the Hillsboro College tennis coach sharing an intimate little dinner with a player from the tour. The player caught Alie's eye and nodded at her.

"Is it a problem, her being here?" I asked.

"No. I know about her, she knows about me. I've run into her at places like this before."

Big Holly returned. "Something to drink?"

"I'm kind of still on duty," I said. "Better just bring me an Evian, Holly."

"Same for me," Alie said with a sheepish smile that acknowledged she'd already had enough.

"Food?" Big Holly asked. Alie shrugged, so Holly said, "I'll bring you some hors d'oeuvres. You can nibble."

We were as alone as you can be in a roomful of people. Alie looked at me. I looked at Alie. I was out of my league.

"You were very brave," Alie said.

"Nah. I'm a cop. I did what I was supposed to."

"I mean it, Kotter." She clasped my hand.

I felt the electricity shooting up my arm and arcing speedily to all the places that made me want to do whatever it took to please someone like Alie. I became very conscious of Alie's body stretched against the silky fabric of her shirt, and I imagined how those jeans must be curved against her as she leaned forward in her chair. The music seemed particularly sultry as it swirled around us, and I found myself blurting, "Dance?"

Her smile had a little triumph in it. The control was swinging back her way. We went to the dance floor.

I held her close, alive with the sensation of her breasts against me. Traces of the alcohol and smoke that poisoned the atmosphere at Poe's still clung to her, but I was a creature of the gutter and did not care. I wondered whether she could feel my trembling as we swayed sensually to the music.

When the song ended, we returned to the table. My throat was so tight, I couldn't trust myself to speak. Alie folded herself back into her own thoughts. We sat in silence, picking at the food Big Holly brought us. After awhile, Alie asked me to take her back to the College Inn. She rode in the back seat, still not talking.

At the hotel she closed the door to her room without saying good night. It didn't matter. I had danced with her, and that was enough.

CHAPTER ELEVEN

When the telephone rang in the morning, I was already awake, puttering around in sweatpants and a T-shirt. It was a miracle.

"Hello, Kotter speaking," I said, very politely.

I heard Randie laugh. "You're a quick study, aren't you?"

"Good morning, Captain."

"Are you up?"

"Yeah."

"I'm calling from the lobby. I'll be right there."

I figured Randie's visit must be Julie's doing, unexpected as it was. The voyeur in me wondered what had been offered or withheld in the night to bring it about.

Randie appeared in her uniform with a couple of takeout cups of coffee and the *Courier*. "Have you seen the paper yet?"

Penn's story on Papa de Ville was plastered across the front page, and it was a good one. Penn had done his homework. He even tracked down an old assistant principal, retired to the Home of Merciful Rest, a name that always sounded more like a cemetery than a nursing home to me. The assistant principal had helped to discipline the schoolboy gambling ring and recalled Papa as "wild and unrepentant."

Penn also had a quote from Alie's agent insisting Papa's past had nothing to do with the recent mugging. "Do you believe that?" I asked.

"Not in the least. Let's see if anybody else is talking about this," Randie said, flipping on the television.

Somebody else sure was. Not only were the local news stations repeating the story, but it was all over ESPN. The sports network already was pronouncing Papa to be one of those Rotten Tennis Dads, like the fathers of Steffi Graf or Mary Pierce.

"I think this tournament is about to get a little more media attention. What do you think, Kotter?" Randie deadpanned.

"The mayor said it would give Hillsboro a new identity."

We watched the ESPN broadcast until it moved

on to the baseball scores. Randie hit the "mute" button and said, "So how did it go last night? Did she still want to go to Poe's?"

"She did."

"Any problems?"

"Nothing to speak of."

"Are you telling me the truth?"

She always knew. Since I was a kid tagging along with her softball teams, Randie had always known. I shrugged.

"Did you do anything that could get you in trouble?" she asked.

"You know," I said, "when you go into a night with the rules turned upside down, it almost has to happen, doesn't it?"

"All right," Randie said. "All right."

She didn't ask me anything else. I would have told her if she did, but this way it became one of those moments of friendship you never forget.

"The detectives have tracked down some of the names from Papa de Ville's old gambling ring," Randie said. "One guy's dead, another one's been in jail for years in California, one just had a heart transplant and is still in the hospital, and one of them's a truck driver who's on the road a lot. They even found one guy who never lost the gambling bug — he's a security guard in an Atlantic City casino."

"They better watch the till," I said.

"Don't you know it. A lot of the rest of the crew are apparently still in the area, but they're the types who go from apartment to apartment, job to job and woman to woman. The detectives are having the usual trouble finding them, and of course, our

130

culprits are probably among them. Still, the investigation is going pretty well."

"Thanks to Penn."

"Yeah. As if that hasn't happened before."

We passed the time until the door across the hallway was flung open. "Kotter! Do you know what the fuck is going on?" Alie said, the voice at full throttle.

She came busting over, sexy as always in shorts and a sweatshirt, then spotted Randie and stopped in her tracks. A wary expression came over her, and it was pretty obvious she was trying to figure out whether there was something going on between Randie and me. "I didn't expect you'd have company at this hour."

"Don't worry," I said drily. "I'm not trying to sleep my way to the top."

"In Kotter's case, even that wouldn't help," Randie added wittily.

Alie giggled. "I remember you. You're Captain Wilkes, right? You came here the night my father got mugged when they wanted to put all that extra security around me."

"Instead, you got Kotter," Randie said, smiling.

"Yeah. Hey, Kotter, how come you never wear your uniform? Captain Wilkes looks great in hers."

Three new suits — two that Randie knew about — and this babe wishes I was in uniform. I couldn't believe it. Randie would never let me forget this. I didn't dare look at her. I'm sure it was all she could do to keep from laughing.

Oblivious to the destruction she was sowing, Alie plunged ahead. "Kotter, what's going on? My agent just called and said to make sure I don't talk to any reporters. I'm supposed to go over and meet with him and my father." She glanced at Randie, then went ahead, anyway. "Did anyone find out about the Hollies?"

"I think they probably want to talk about what was in the paper this morning," I said and handed it to her.

Alie read Penn's story — without moving her lips. "That's horrible! It was so long ago! How come the press has to go and dig up things like that? Oh well. At least it has nothing to do with what happened to us." She smiled at Randie. "Kotter was awesome. Did she tell you?"

Oh God. In my darkest nightmares I could not have anticipated this.

"Kotter's so modest," Randie said smoothly. "Maybe you better tell me."

Alie turned out to be a pretty lurid storyteller, even if she had to ask for help at the crucial part. "Then Kotter came running up, and she told the guy to stop, but he told her to go fuck herself, so she took out, you know, one of those little clubs —"

"A blackjack?" Randie prompted.

"Yeah, a blackjack." Alie charged through the rest of the story, including our visit to the Hollies, although she didn't mention the dance.

"Thanks for telling me," Randie said.

"Well, you should know. I mean, Kotter really saved me. Anyway, I have to get ready for my meeting. See you in a few, Kotter." She bounced back across the hall and shut the door.

I was cooked. Visions of internal affairs danced in my head. "Guilty as charged," I said softly.

Randie looked at me for such a long time I thought my heart would stop. Then she said, "You know, Kotter, maybe we'll just add this to the long list of reasons why you owe me your soul."

"Randie, my soul ain't worth that much."

"Then you're getting the better part of the bargain, aren't you?"

"I always have."

"Just be sure you remember that. Well, it's time for me to get to the station, and you need to take Alie out to her father's condo. And, Kotter?"

"What?"

"Give the girl a thrill. Go ahead and wear your uniform."

For the record, I did not wear my uniform to drive Alie to Buena Vista and Papa de Ville's condo. My fellow officers were out there, and no self-respecting cop ever puts on a uniform when she has the option to dress in civilian clothes. I would look like a dork in uniform, and I wasn't going to do that, even for Alie. I put on the blue suit.

Alie appeared in jeans and one of those sleeveless, cropped T-shirts that showed off her taut and tanned midsection. I nodded my appreciation, and she smiled knowingly. After last night, after the heroics and the dance, there was no denying the sexual tension between us.

"Don't you wish," she teased.

"Wish for what?"

She didn't bother to answer. She had me, and she knew it. In life or on a tennis court, Alie de Ville wasn't happy unless she was dictating the play.

At Buena Vista I joined the security detail at the condo. Alie stayed through lunchtime, and then I took her back to the College Inn. There was a message waiting for me to call Randie.

"Wilkes here."

"It's Kotter. You called?"

"Yeah, I thought you'd want to know this. I went over to Charlie's to pick up a sandwich for lunch, and they had the WHLL sports talk show on the radio. The Hillsboro College football fans are in mourning. There's a new freshman linebacker named Shawn Bevan who was supposed to be the hope of the defense, but he's hurt and they don't know when he'll be able to play. Apparently he suffered a freak elbow accident in practice yesterday, but he didn't notice it until it swelled up on him last night."

"Really."

"You're in the clear, Kotter. It never happened."

"Thanks, Randie."

"Everything going okay today?"

"So far."

"Be alert at the tournament tonight. If anybody wants to hurt Papa or Alie, Penn's story is the sort of thing that can spook them into trying something desperate."

* * * * *

134

The tournament was a mob scene of reporters. They weren't interested when it was just some little hick event, but the news about Papa de Ville changed all of that.

Papa, of course, was furious. He had been miffed when the press was minimal, but now he wanted it to go away. Papa should have learned the lesson I did: *Be careful what you wish for. Sometimes you need to be specific.*

Alie departed from her routine, staying at the College Inn as late as she could to try to avoid the media horde. Sam Van Doren helped me get her from the cruiser through a gauntlet of reporters to the locker room. Alie kept her eyes down and ignored the shouted questions.

I took up my courtside post and scanned the crowded bleachers. There's nothing like scandal to pull the people in. The only empty seats in the place were in Papa de Ville's box. He finally rushed in just moments before Alie finished her warmup. The mayor was with him, and so were a couple of cops.

It was the semifinal round. Alie's opponent was Maria Lopez, another young player ranked in the Top 10 with a dazzling array of shots.

Maria served first and began the match with a blistering ace. On the next serve, Alie cracked off a clean winner. It was quite an exchange of calling cards, and the crowd was humming. This one was going to be a sizzler.

Maria and Alie had beautifully contrasting styles. Alie had that classic serve-and-volley game, and Maria had the pinpoint passing shots to challenge it. Their rivalry had the potential to last for years, and so neither one was willing to concede anything, even in a dinky little tournament that didn't count for anything in the rankings.

The first set went to a tiebreaker. The winner of it would be the one who got to seven points first, except she had to win by two, and neither player was having any luck coming up with that much of an edge. The score went to 7–7, then 8–8, 9–9 and 10–10, the crowd howling on every point.

It was so intense, with the referee pleading for quiet to no avail, that maybe the two cops near Papa de Ville could be excused a little for being surprised when a burly figure barreled around them and launched himself recklessly at Papa de Ville, getting his hands around Papa's neck in a choke hold that meant business.

This was it! Every cop and security guard in the place became focused on the man grappling with Papa — everyone, that is, except me. An uncommon realization came over me, that maybe this was it, or maybe this was just a diversion and the real target was . . .

Alie.

I climbed over the low wall separating me from the tennis court. Alie and Maria had stopped playing. Alie stood transfixed, watching the attack on her father. I was running toward her as fast as I could, running even before I saw the two men charging toward her with a head start that would get them to her before I could.

Alie had her back to them, and there was no way she could hear any shout of warning in all of the pandemonium.

I changed directions, sprinting now not to reach Alie but to intercept the men if I could. It was the only chance I had to save her. I had my gun, but it was useless. If they got to her before I did, she would be a human shield and I couldn't fire. Anyway, there was too much risk of shooting someone in the crowd.

I ran fast, fast, fast, faster than Alie's assailants, angling in behind them as they stormed toward her. I lunged, catapulting my entire body into the air, smashing against the back of the knees of the one who was a little farther behind. He stumbled heavily against his accomplice, and the two of them fell clumsily to the ground. A stray, very absurd thought flashed through my mind, that I had brought them down with an illegal clip. Well, I would deal with the fifteen-yard penalty later.

I scrambled to my feet before they could, drew my gun and aimed it at them in the pose they teach you in the police academy.

"Move and I'll blow your motherfucking heads off!" I screamed.

I don't know whether they heard me in the suffocating noise, but it didn't matter. In seconds I was surrounded by other cops, assuring me everything was okay, crushing knees into the backs of the two thugs and handcuffing them. All around me cops were mouthing the Miranda rights like a mass telling of the rosary.

I was actually out of the picture, until Alie came racing for me like a doe in flight. She was crying hysterically as she flung herself against me. "Kotter, Kotter, Kotter, Kotter!" she beseeched me.

I held her tight. I don't know what I said —

137

whatever came into my head — to try to calm her down. Her tears wet my cheek and collar.

After a time, some of the cops came and gently separated us. We wound up in different police cars, the sirens screaming in the night.

Everything was a blur until I found myself in Randie's office with the door closed, just her and me, and I stopped gasping for air and began simply breathing again.

CHAPTER TWELVE

By the time I got to Randie's office, every single
television station seemed to be showing the footage of
me slicing into Alie's attackers with my unsportsman-
like blocking, while in the background a small army
of cops was wrestling with the goon who jumped
Papa de Ville.

They showed it in real time. They showed it in
slow motion. They followed it with the newly made
mug shots of the three thugs we had under heavy
guard in the cells in the basement of the police
station.

The stories they broadcast along with the footage were unusually accurate, thanks to the legwork Jonnie Penn had done for them.

The three low-lifes we had in custody were indeed members of Papa de Ville's schoolboy gambling ring with a grudge to settle. The reason the detectives hadn't found them is they had gone out of town to set up a daring escapade of revenge.

Their names were Angelo Clemente, Nick Schultz and Myron "Moose" Moore. Clemente was the one who went after Papa de Ville in his seat, and the other two were the ones I intercepted.

They confessed quickly. They hated Papa. Years ago, when they were kicked out of school, the four of them turned to small-time crime together. They pooled their take, which included a couple thousand dollars from the gambling ring. Then Papa got ambition. He phoned in an anonymous tip to the police, ratting out his cronies, stole the stash and lit out of town. Clemente, Schultz and Moore did time while Papa lived it up on their ill-gotten gains. When it was gone, he alternated between petty crime and dead-end jobs until he struck it rich with his miracle glue.

Life grubbed along for Clemente, Schultz and Moore. They spent most of it in bars, some of it in jail and all of it dodging ex-wives and creditors. Then they heard Papa de Ville was coming back to town with his tennis tournament.

"We didn't plan to hurt nobody," Moose Moore said in his confession. "We just thought de Ville owed us a little something, and he wouldn't miss it none. Nick and me went to talk to him the night of the banquet, just friendly-like, but he got mean and started shoving us around. That's when we beat him up."

Papa recognized them, all right, but he didn't want anybody to know he did, because he didn't want his past dredged up. Jonnie Penn would fix that for him, though.

The three confederates weren't ready to give up. They tried to loosen Papa up by sending the threatening note about Alie, but that didn't work, either, so they decided to try something desperate. They figured they would kidnap Alie right off the tennis court.

Clemente would attack Papa to distract everyone. Then Schultz and Moore would grab Alie. They knew Clemente would get nabbed, but once they had Alie, they would demand his release. Then they were going to ask for a car to take them to the airport, a plane and a pilot and three million dollars in cash. Once they got the plane, the pilot and the money, they planned to leave Alie behind and head for the wild blue yonder.

They had scouted out an abandoned airstrip in northern New Jersey, where they had a car waiting. Once they landed, they expected to make their way to New York City and lose themselves among its millions of people.

It was just about crazy enough to work. It might have, if they had managed to grab Alie.

Their story was sensational. It was flashed around the globe, making a disgrace of Papa. Meanwhile, the police station was bedlam. As if we didn't have enough to do, sorting out the most electrifying crime in Hillsboro's history, we were overrun by FBI agents, local politicians trying to horn in on the glory and enough media types to cover a presidential campaign.

The chief and the mayor held a press conference, and I got dragged into it. Suddenly I was their best pal, when just the day before they were ready to part me from my badge. I sweated in the hot camera lights and said as little as possible, giving one- or two-word answers if I couldn't avoid a question. I was the sardonic cop if ever there was one.

I beat it out of there as soon as I could — which was fine with the mayor and the chief, who were quite content to have the limelight to themselves. I wasn't done, though. Randie brought me to The Rathole, where she had parked Jonnie Penn.

"He's entitled to a little more than a press conference," Randie said. "After all, he cracked this case."

I had never done an interview before. I had never wanted to do one, because I always figured if the press wanted to talk to me, it would be because I had done something really bad. I never dreamed of being a hero, and I wasn't even sure I wanted to be.

Still, if Randie wanted me to talk to Penn, I would do it. She stayed to help, and between Randie and Penn, they drew out of me what Penn needed for a heart-warming story of a local kid who became a cop, thanks to the Police Softball League and a coach who cared.

It would be all over the newspaper the next day — the interview, a picture of me standing over Schultz and Moore with my gun pointed at them, and even an old photo of the championship softball team that Randie let Penn borrow. There I was, kneeling in the front row, the only white kid and the only one not smiling.

Finally, my part of the sideshow was over. I was safely tucked away in Randie's office, sipping coffee and trying to get my bearings again. "Where's Alie?" I said.

"Sam took a statement from her and then took her back to the College Inn. She's in her room. My guess is, she'll be leaving in the morning. The rest of the tournament's been canceled, as you can well imagine."

"And Papa?"

"Holed up in his condo, hiding from the press and refusing to talk to us until his lawyer shows. I'd like to see the son of a bitch arrested, but the statute of limitations ran out long ago on anything he did when he lived here."

"Well, the press will get him."

"Yeah. They should make his life miserable for a long time to come," Randie said. "But the hell with him. How are you doing, Kotter?"

"I don't know. This doesn't seem real."

"You're a genuine hero, you know."

"Not me. I'm not the type."

"It's not something you get to choose. Other people do it for you."

"Randie, I swear, I was just scared to death of fucking up out there."

She chuckled then. As usual, the mirth went right through to my soul. I closed my eyes and sighed for the ages, and then Randie pulled me from the chair and gave me a hug I could live on for the rest of my life.

"Do you want to stay with Julie and me tonight?" she said.

"I don't know. I can't seem to make any decisions. Let me get my things from the inn and think about it."

"Whatever you want, Kotter. If you decide to come over, just give us a call. It doesn't matter how late it is."

"Thanks, Randie."

"Kotter?"

"What?"

"I love you, you know."

"Yeah. God knows why. And I love you back."

I ran into Sam Van Doren in the lobby of the College Inn. "Aren't you off this detail yet?" he teased.

"I think I am. I'm just getting my things."

"I guess we're all pretty much done with security. After all, the crooks are in jail. There's just a few of us hanging around in case some crazy decides to try something with Allie. You heading home?"

"Probably. But I'm so tired, I'm liable to fall into that bed up there and not bother."

"You did good, Kotter."

"Thanks, Sam. It means something coming from you."

I went upstairs to my room and started shoving stuff into my bag. The telephone rang, and I really didn't want to answer it, but I figured I better, in case it was Randie.

It wasn't. "Kotter, get over here," Alie said.

I was worn out. I didn't want to see her. I didn't want to see anybody, but she hung up before I could say anything. I went across the hall and pushed open the unlocked door.

She was lounging in the front room in a long robe of pink silk, which draped her as exquisitely as a goddess. I stopped and swayed as though I'd been hit by lightning. I don't know what I expected, but it wasn't this. The last time I saw her, she was crying like a child.

"Kotter, I hurt my shoulder in the match tonight. I can't unhook my necklace. Will you do it?"

She wasn't fooling anybody with that line about her shoulder, but I didn't particularly care. I went behind her, fingered the clasp to her gold necklace and deliberately fumbled with it. I had a wonderful vantage point, and I took my time admiring the view, gazing at the breasts I could see all the way to their nipples inside the folds of the pink silk robe.

By and by I unhooked the necklace and let go of it, watching it slither between her breasts and puddle there. Slowly I slid my hand after it, but as I got to Alie's chest, she reached up and stopped me. She took my hand and drew me around in front of her, then used my arm to draw me in and offered me her upturned lips.

We kissed, the pent-up passion exploding between us and sending wave after wave of erotic shocks through my body. I was drowning in this. My hands slid down the silk to her waist, but she broke off the kiss and pushed me away.

"Just use your mouth on me," she said feverishly.

She stood up, and the gold necklace fell to the floor. She undid her silk sash and held it out. "Turn around and put your hands behind your back."

There was too much of the cop in me for that. "No," I said.

"Yes," she said, the word seductive and — God help me — irresistible. "It's not for real, Kotter. It's only a game. I won't tie it tight. I promise."

"All right."

She looped the sash lightly around my hands. The robe fell away from her, showing me the perfect form I had craved since the moment I saw her standing on the curb outside the airport terminal. There was not a blemish upon her. Her cheekbones, collar bones and rib cage were delicate structures beneath the smooth skin that was so much silkier than any robe. Her muscles were cords of majesty, her stomach as flat as her hips were curved. My eyes roamed everywhere, but I stared longest and hardest at the inviting triangle of light and curly hair.

"Come here," she said as she sat back in her chair.

Once again we kissed, and now that I could not touch her with my hands, my lips searched her out in wild hunger. Maybe there was something to this sash around my wrists, after all.

I left her mouth and kissed my way gently down her neck, lingering at the bewitching hollows. I had not had my fill when she enticed me elsewhere, cupping her breasts in her own hands and offering them up. They were small and firm, and they gave my eager mouth a choice of soft curves or darkening, hardening buds. I feasted there as she moaned and muttered, "This one . . . now the other one . . . oh, go back . . . yes, the other one again . . ."

She squirmed in the chair as I moved on to kiss the taut midriff that had tantalized me for days. I spent much time there, while her fingers teased her own breasts and she pleaded with me, "Keep going, keep going, keep going."

I made her wait and wait and wait, but eventually I could stand it no longer. I wanted the mystery of her. As I brushed my mouth through the light curls, she spread wide for me, and with a deep breath I plunged in.

I lost myself in the taste and scent of her, in the dark honeycombs and swells that beckoned me. Oh, I had all the time in the world now, I was the giver of earthly delights, and she would know madness before I was done.

She gripped the chair. She laced her fingers in my hair and pressed her nails into my skin. She begged. She cursed. She groaned in sweet agony. Then she arched and bucked and writhed and shouted as I gave the bitch what she wanted.

She sagged in her chair. I stood swiftly, ripping the sash from my hands, and caught her up in a ravishing kiss. We were both sweaty and heaving, lovers of conquest, not of tenderness.

When she regained her strength, she shoved me away and held me spellbound with sultry eyes. My fists were clenched. I waited upon her.

"Go and turn on the Jacuzzi," she said.

I did as I was told. She came in and dropped the

robe on the cool tiles, then slowly submerged her luscious body in the warm, churning waters. She caressed her nipples and taunted me with a smile. I looked at her with ravaging desire.

"All right," she said. "You can come in now."

I started to take off the jacket to my blue suit, but she spoke again. "No. Come in as you are. Leave your clothes on."

My best suit! I looked at her in frustration, but what the hell. She was worth ruining a new suit for. I splashed in.

She laughed triumphantly and kissed me, her hands playing roughly with my breasts through my shirt. She used her strong legs to knock me off balance and pushed me under the water. When I came up sputtering and coughing, the water stinging my eyes, I felt her yank off the button on my trousers and pull down the zipper. She pinned me against the side of the Jacuzzi, and her hand went into my crotch. Her mouth crushed against mine, the water swirled around me, the heat rose in steamy vapors, and she fucked me as though she owned me and I was there for the taking.

When she was done with me, I collapsed. It was all I could do to hold myself out of the water.

She left me there, got out and calmly toweled herself off. After a moment I pulled myself shakily out of the Jacuzzi. Alie helped me strip off my sopping clothes.

I left them in a heap. I knew I would never wear them again. Randie was going to see that new green suit, after all, damn her eyes.

Naked, we went into the bedroom and got

between the sheets. We had so much more lovemaking to do.

Later in the night I stirred. I didn't entirely come to, just enough to realize that through it all, not once had I noticed Alie's ungodly voice.

EPILOGUE

In the morning I was awakened by the sensation of Alie's hands running lightly over my body. Believe me, there are worse ways to wake up.

She smiled at me dreamily. "I've got to go to New York for the U.S. Open. I want you to come with me."

"I don't know," I said, but she started doing things to me that made it impossible to say no.

We made love, and then I telephoned Randie. Just

in case I was wavering, Alie got on her knees and licked my belly and thighs and crooned obscenities explaining what else she wanted to do to me.

Randie was understanding. "You've got vacation left for the year, and you're entitled to some leave after what you went through this week. Take all the time you want, Kotter."

"I'll miss you," I said.

"Kotter, go explore the world. There's a lot to life outside Hillsboro."

That afternoon I flew out with Alie on a private jet. I didn't bring a suitcase. She said we'd get what I needed as we went along.

We had an incredible time together, and it didn't hurt that Alie was playing great tennis. Maybe the two went together. Anyway, she got through the quarterfinals by beating her arch-rival Maria Lopez, then lost in the semifinals in three sensational sets to Monica Seles.

The U.S. Open is always a media circus, and it was worse for Alie than usual because of what happened in Hillsboro. Still, she stonewalled the press pretty effectively, and the tournament officials protected her. Papa de Ville never showed, which was a great relief.

Three weeks after I left Hillsboro, I made my way back and walked into the police station as evening was coming on.

All was quiet. The Beer Belly Polka was at his post.

"Kotter?" he said. "Christ, where have you been? You look like you've been on a binge for weeks!"

"Sarge, I've been in a place so strange that even you look good to me," I said and planted a big smackeroo on his forehead.

"Kotter, for Christ sakes!" he bellowed, but he was bright red and looking rather pleased.

I went to Randie's office and turned myself in. Her eyes lighted up at the sight of me, then did a quick inventory to see that I was all right. "What hap- pened, Kotter?" she asked, a lilt in her voice. "Did she wear you out?"

"She sure as hell tried."

"But you were up to the challenge."

"It's true. I was up to the challenge."

"Well, your talents were never in doubt — only your judgment."

"Great. I've been back for two minutes, and look what I get. I'm just another one of those battered people who can't stop going back to abusive relationships."

"Are you back?"

"Yeh."

"It wasn't working out?"

"It was working out fine," I said. "It was terrific. We had intimate little dinners, went to all kinds of parties and hung out with a bunch of celebrities. I even got to meet Martina. Money was no object. Alie bought whatever I wanted and even some things I didn't particularly want but she wanted for me. And the babe has an incredible imagination in the sack. She plays a game of 'Simon Says' you wouldn't believe. It was the high life, for sure."

"So?"

"So there were the coach and the trainer and the agent and Papa on the phone all the time and the

152

officials from the women's tennis tour and the sponsors and the press and the groupies. It was Camp de Ville out there, and I wasn't cut out for it. I didn't want to be indentured to her, you know?"

"That's because you're already apprenticed to me."

"I guess so."

Randie came around her desk. She draped her arm affectionately and protectively around my shoulders. It was supposed to make me feel good, and it always did. "Come on," she said. "Let's go to the Hollies. Just you and me. With your talents, there's someone else out there already, just waiting for you. And Kotter?"

"What?"

"I'm glad you're home."

A few of the publications of
THE NAIAD PRESS, INC.
P.O. Box 10543 • Tallahassee, Florida 32302
Phone (904) 539-5965
Toll-Free Order Number: 1-800-533-1973
Mail orders welcome. Please include 15% postage.
Write or call for our free catalog which also features an
incredible selection of lesbian videos.

COURTED by Celia Cohen. 160 pp. Sparkling romantic
encounter.   ISBN 1-56280-166-X $11.95

SEASONS OF THE HEART by Jackie Calhoun. 240 pp. Romance
through the years.   ISBN 1-56280-167-8   11.95

K. C. BOMBER by Janet McClellan. 208 pp. 1st Tru North
mystery.   ISBN 1-56280-157-0   11.95

LAST RITES by Tracey Richardson. 192 pp. 1st Stevie Houston
mystery.   ISBN 1-56280-164-3   11.95

EMBRACE IN MOTION by Karin Kallmaker. 256 pp. A whirlwind
love affair.   ISBN 1-56280-165-1   11.95

HOT CHECK by Peggy J. Herring. 192 pp. Will workaholic Alice
fall for guitarist Ricky?   ISBN 1-56280-163-5   11.95

OLD TIES by Saxon Bennett. 176 pp. Can Cleo surrender to a
passionate new love?   ISBN 1-56280-159-7   11.95

LOVE ON THE LINE by Laura DeHart Young. 176 pp. Will Stef win Kay's
heart?   ISBN 1-56280-162-7 $11.95

DEVIL'S LEG CROSSING by Kaye Davis. 192 pp. 1st Maris Middleton
mystery.   ISBN 1-56280-158-9   11.95

COSTA BRAVA by Marta Balletbo Coll. 144 pp. Read the book,
see the movie!   ISBN 1-56280-153-8   11.95

MEETING MAGDALENE & OTHER STORIES by
Marilyn Freeman. 144 pp. Read the book, see the movie!
                                                     ISBN 1-56280-170-8   11.95

These are just a few of the many Naiad Press titles — we are the oldest and
largest lesbian/feminist publishing company in the world. We also offer an
enormous selection of lesbian video products. Please request a complete
catalog. We offer personal service; we encourage and welcome direct mail
orders from individuals who have limited access to bookstores carrying our
publications.